The Locket's *Secret*

By K. Kelley Heyne

Pauline
BOOKS & MEDIA
Boston

Library of Congress Cataloging-in-Publication Data

Heyne, K. Kelley.
 The locket's secret / by K. Kelley Heyne.
  p. cm.
 Summary: Faced with devastating feelings of loss after the death of her
sister and having to move away from her home, thirteen-year-old Carrie
escapes into a fantasy world, despite her family's efforts to draw her back
to them.
 ISBN-13: 978-0-8198-7484-9
 ISBN-10: 0-8198-7484-1
 [1. Grief--Fiction. 2. Moving, Household--Fiction. 3. Family life--Fiction. 4.
Christian life--Fiction. 5. Catholics--Fiction. 6. Home schooling--Fiction.] I.
Title.
 PZ7.H478Loc 2013
 [Fic]--dc23
                                2012027872

This is a work of fiction. Names, characters, places, events, and incidents are either
the products of the author's imagination or used in a fictitious manner. Any resem-
blance to actual persons, living or dead, or actual events is purely coincidental.

Many manufacturers and sellers distinguish their products through the use of trademarks. Any trademark designations that appear in this book are used in good faith
but are not authorized by, associated with, or sponsored by the trademark owners.

Cover design by Mary Joseph Peterson, FSP
Cover photo by Mary Emmanuel Alves, FSP
Thank you to Monica Marsh for serving as the model for the cover photo.

All rights reserved. No part of this book may be reproduced or transmitted
in any form or by any means, electronic or mechanical, including pho-
tocopying, recording, or by any information storage and retrieval system,
without permission in writing from the publisher.

"P" and PAULINE are registered trademarks of the Daughters of St. Paul.

Copyright © 2013, K. Kelley Heyne

Published by Pauline Books & Media, 50 Saint Pauls Avenue, Boston, MA
02130-3491

Printed in the U.S.A.

TLS VSAUSAPEOILL1-4J13-00068 7484-1

www.pauline.org

Pauline Books & Media is the publishing house of the Daughters of St. Paul,
an international congregation of women religious serving the Church with
the communications media.

1 2 3 4 5 6 7 8 9   17 16 15 14 13

To Mom, with love.

Contents

Chapter 1

C arrie stared glumly out the van's window. The view was gorgeous and ever-changing, but she could not enjoy it. Every mile the van traveled took her further from her home, her room, her friends, and the mountain scenery she loved. No more mountains, no more beaches.

No more Meg.

She and Meg had belonged to the same homeschool group back in Bremerton, Washington. Now she had lost the one friend she felt like she had anything in common with. The only one who read the same books, listened to the same music, dreamed the same dreams.

Carrie sighed. How could there ever be anyone like Meg in her life, ever again?

Ever since they had left Washington, Carrie had refused to wear anything in her long brown hair except the headband that Meg had made for her as a going-away present. Her friend had glued rosettes, rhinestones, and ribbons to a plastic head-band. It wasn't really Carrie's style, but she wore it anyway. Now she adjusted it in her hair and turned up the volume on her MP3 player, refusing to listen to the music playing in the van.

"Carrie?"

Carrie pretended not to hear her mother calling her.

"Carrie? Carrie!"

Mrs. Adams's voice grew more insistent. Carrie sighed and paused her music, pulling out her earbuds. She looked up at her mother without speaking. She hadn't spoken much to her parents since they had made the decision to move.

It was her mother's turn to sigh and shake her head. Carrie felt a twinge of guilt, but she pushed it away.

"Carrie, we're going to stop for lunch soon. Would you rather help with Sammy, or help your dad unload?"

"I'll help Sammy," she said grudgingly, glancing at her youngest brother. Sammy clapped cheerfully and threw a fruit snack at her. Then he went back to drawing a picture. He was drawing faces again, the same group of six faces he always drew whenever he drew people. He had also drawn an "S" several times. It was one of the only letters he knew. Carrie's other brother, Jonny, was playing a video game, but he looked up, caught her eye, and smiled. What she saw as a dreary road trip, he saw as an adventure. She turned her head to look back out the window, replacing her earbuds and grimacing.

She'd already had enough of this trip and there were still three whole days to go.

She gazed off into space.

She was astride a black steed called Midnight. The chink of the harness and the steady clip-clop of hooves were the only sounds under the dense canopy arching over the forest track. She checked the knife at her belt to be sure it was loose in its sheath. These woods were dangerous, and she would not be caught empty-handed.

The broad-shouldered man at the head of the column raised his hand, stopping the cavalcade. He reined his steed around and brought his horse close to Caritas's.

"My lady, night is falling fast. We must make camp soon," he informed her with an air of authority.

"Not yet, Ryan. We can press on a few miles more. We must make speed while we can," Caritas answered anxiously as she glanced back at the makeshift parade of soldiers, servants, her brothers, and . . . no, just her brothers. "Just a bit farther today, Ryan. We can all rest when we reach our destination."

"What?" Carrie snapped back to reality to find her father staring at her in bewilderment. She hadn't realized that she was murmuring the last part of her daydream out loud.

"Carrie, I asked if you wanted to stretch your legs. Your mom and your brothers are eating lunch at the picnic table. I need to fill the gas tank. We might not be stopping again till we reach the hotel," he said. The wrinkle above his nose deepened a little with worry as he asked, "Are you okay?"

She dropped her eyes and answered, "I'm fine. I'll eat here."

Jonny and Mom were walking outside with Sammy. Mom bent her pregnant figure to see what he was holding up to show her. *Probably a bug,* Carrie thought. Mom was smiling. Everyone seemed oblivious to the fact that they had left their lives behind in Washington. Everyone seemed happy for the "fresh start," as Mom called it with a painful smile. Everyone but Carrie.

Soon they were on the road again, merging into the speeding freeway traffic. Carrie, tired of watching the passing fields and trees, thought about her options. She could nap, but she wasn't sleepy. She could snack, but she wasn't hungry or thirsty. She ached. Ached from being in the van hour after hour. Ached from having slept in an unfamiliar bed the night before. Ached from boredom. Ached from loneliness. She closed her gray eyes.

Caritas faced Ryan across the space between their horses. She was tense and, as she so often did when she was nervous or disturbed, she fingered her heart-shaped locket. It was smooth and cool and hard. The forest was growing darker, but they could still travel. They needed to press on to their destination. They needed to put this journey behind them. Her burly bodyguard looked hesitant to obey her decision. Then he remembered his place and signaled the caravan forward. The pack animals, soldiers, and servants fell into line again and moved forward. The steeds carrying her brothers cantered behind her own horse. At this pace they would make a few more miles before nightfall.

Then the silence under the trees was shattered.

Armed men leaped out from the shadows under the trees and attacked the party. A few of the guard fell wounded. Some of the soldiers and servants bolted into the forest. A loud voice called the attackers to stand down. One mounted figure had an arrow trained right at Caritas.

"Princess, please tell your retinue to drop their arms. I would hate to kill more of them than absolutely necessary."

Behind her Caritas could hear Jonathon comforting Samuel. Their horses stood flank to flank and the older boy had his arm around the younger protectively. She let her eyes dwell briefly on the opposing forces frozen around her. Her retinue had only a handful of soldiers and servants left, and they were now outnumbered at least two to one. Ryan looked grim.

"You'll never get away with this, Mort. My father will

send an army after us. You and your band will hang for this," she said between clenched teeth.

Mort, well-known to Caritas as a member of her uncle Frederick's circle, was a tall, handsome man whose courtly air could not conceal his malevolent character. He smiled widely at her threat. He had his prey. He wasn't worried about repercussions.

In the midst of the tense standoff, Caritas met Ryan's eyes for a moment and she nodded ever so slightly. He nodded back.

Without warning, Caritas dug her heels into the flanks of her horse, driving her spurs in hard. With a scream, Midnight reared and plunged at the unexpected and unmerited punishment. The horse's wild reaction took him close to Mort's horse, which reared and backed away nervously. Caritas kept her seat with difficulty as the shouts around her only made Midnight struggle more. Finally, one of the brigands dismounted and managed to catch the bridle of the frightened horse. Midnight slowly calmed. Caritas, with hair disheveled but still in her saddle, gazed at Mort impassively. A small smile played on one side of her mouth.

"Missing something, Mort?" she asked with feigned innocence.

Mort, suddenly suspicious, took stock of the captured party. He let out a howl of rage, causing Midnight to start and shy again.

Ryan was gone. Jonathon and Samuel were also gone. The diversion had worked and her brothers were safe.

"I warned you that you'd never get away with it. My brothers are with the best woodsman that ever lived. They have miles of forest to hide in. You'll never find them." She could not resist boasting. She had saved them.

"Carrie? We're here," Mr. Adams announced.

Carrie shook her head slightly to clear it. She pulled her brown hair into a loose ponytail and dropped her hand to her locket to make sure it was still there. Sometimes she felt happier in her daydreams than she did in real life. She didn't hurt so much in them, for one thing, and her best friend stayed close by. In her daydream her brothers were safe—not like in real life, where people were not always safe . . . like Cecilia. But she shuddered quickly away from that train of thought. She felt a lot less bitter about life in general in her daydream.

As she carried both Sammy and her backpack into the hotel, she noticed the standard hotel swimming pool. She also noted, as her dad checked them in, that they had the standard size room—again. She gritted her teeth. It was impossible to have time to yourself when you were sharing one large room with four other people. She usually coped by keeping her earbuds in and her nose buried in one of her favorite books.

"Hey, wanna do cannonballs in the pool later? Bet I can splash bigger than you," Jonny's chatter broke into her reverie. He was making faces at Sammy, causing the little boy to giggle.

"I dunno. Maybe," she said indifferently. She found it very difficult to be enthusiastic about anything anymore.

After dinner, swimming, and putting Sammy to bed, it was too late to watch a movie on Dad's laptop, so they got ready for bed. Jonny shared a bed with his brother and it was Carrie's turn to sleep on the floor in a sleeping bag. She didn't mind. She had one of the fluffy hotel pillows and a tiny reading light she was allowed to use as long as it didn't keep her brothers awake. They rarely complained, even when she was pretty sure it *did* keep them awake.

She pulled her well-worn wooden rosary out of her backpack. Her uncle had brought it back for her from a pilgrimage to Rome. It had been blessed by the pope. The rough, familiar feel of it in her hand was comforting. She started praying her nightly Rosary. It was a habit, and a comforting one, so she did it. But she didn't feel like praying. It felt like no one was really listening. She didn't understand why God had taken so much from her so quickly. Everything that was familiar was gone now: all her friends, Meg, her home . . . and Cecilia.

Chapter 2

Carrie didn't let herself think about Cecilia during the day. When she did, she invariably started crying. And she couldn't explain why she was crying to her mom without her mom crying too. And that was just too painful for everyone, especially now that they were cooped up in the van for hours.

So Cecilia got locked up in the little place in Carrie's head that she only unlocked at night, when she spread her treasured memories out like a jeweler admiring his wares.

Tonight she remembered their last Halloween, when she and Meg had taken Cecilia out trick-or-treating. All three of them had dressed as princesses, in long gowns and circlet crowns and dress-up jewelry. At five years old, Cecilia was thrilled to be out with the big girls, and she held their hands as she skipped along between houses, unable to contain her excitement. In the dark now, Carrie could almost feel her hand around her sister's and hear her laughter.

Now that the lights were out and everyone was asleep, Carrie let herself cry. For herself, for everything and everyone she missed, but mostly for Cecilia.

She had become good at crying quietly, but she heard her mom shift and sit up.

"Carrie?" she whispered.

Carrie lay still and pretended to be asleep, breathing deeply. She hoped she was convincing. She heard her mom get out of bed and walk over to her. Her ruse hadn't worked.

"Honey, what's wrong?" she asked.

"Nothing," Carrie said into her pillow, hoping that if she muffled her voice, her mother wouldn't hear it break.

"Carrie, I'm so sorry you're unhappy. That's not what we intended when we made the decision to move. You know we had to because your dad was offered a better job at St. Sebastian College. It means more stability and a better salary and . . ."

"A fresh start. I know," Carrie interrupted, with her face still in the pillow.

"Sweetie," her mom said softly, while stroking her hair, "it's so much more complicated than that. We both know that. And . . ." Now Carrie heard the catch in her mom's voice, ". . . we *all* miss her."

Carrie finally sat up, trying hard to speak softly and not break down.

"But it's only been nine months. It feels like we're leaving her. She's alone now," she said franticly.

"No, baby, she's not," her mom said firmly. "She's still with us. Can't you feel that?" Her mother's hand had found her face even in the dark. She knew her mother could feel the tears on her cheeks.

Carrie let go of her rosary and unconsciously reached for her locket. Now the tears were coming freely and there was nothing she could do about it. "Why did God have to take her?" she moaned. "She was so little! It's not right. There should have been so much more time."

Her mom embraced her. Carrie was cradled against her mother, against the bulge of the new baby, oldest and youngest rocked together in their mother's arms. Her mother pressed her face into Carrie's hair and Carrie knew her mother's tears were falling, too.

"Oh, sweetie. It's going to hurt for a long time. I'm so sorry. I wish I could make the pain go away. But I need you to do something for me, for all of us," she said.

"What?" Carrie mumbled into her mother's sleeve.

"We need you to try not to hide your feelings, but to trust us enough to talk to your dad and me. Try to come out of yourself and be part of the family again, so we can help each other. I know it's not going to be easy. But you're stronger than you think. Your family needs you, Carrie," she pleaded.

"I'll . . . I'll try, Mom," she agreed.

"I love you, sweetie."

"Love you, too, Mom."

Her mother kissed the top of her head and held her for a little longer.

"Try to sleep. We've got another long day tomorrow."

"Okay. Thanks, Mom."

"You're welcome."

Carrie's mother returned to bed and Carrie curled up in her sleeping bag. She picked up her rosary and started again with the familiar prayers. Her weariness caught up with her and she fell fast asleep.

❧

The next day she got Sammy dressed and was combing his hair before breakfast. She could tell he was trying not to squirm while she got him ready. He looked at her with his big gray eyes, just a shade darker than hers. He always seemed to see more than a typical three-year-old.

"Silly says hi," he said matter-of-factly.

Carrie froze. "Silly" was what he had called his older sister Cecilia.

"What?" she asked in surprise.

"Silly says hi," he reiterated as if it were the most commonplace thing in the world. His legs swung back and forth off the edge of the chair where he was perched.

"Oh. Um . . . when did she say that?" asked Carrie, feeling very uncomfortable.

"Last night. I saw her. And she said hi," Sammy answered. He was so casual in speaking about his dead sister. His eyes traveled around the room as he tried to keep still.

Carrie's eyes stung with tears that threatened to overwhelm her. She tried to pull herself together.

"Do you see her a lot?" she asked.

"Sometimes," he answered, shrugging his chubby shoulders.

If only he would stop staring at her so innocently.

"You okay, Carrie?" Sammy asked with a concern in his baby face that nearly pushed her over the edge of her grief. She quickly grabbed a few of his toy cars from his bag of clothes. He smiled widely and hugged her impulsively when she presented them.

"I'm all right, Sammy. Let me brush my teeth and we'll get breakfast," she said.

"Okay," he answered as he settled himself down to play with his cars.

So much for keeping it together during the day, Carrie thought bitterly, as she scrubbed the brush roughly over her teeth. How could Sammy be so . . . calm? So casual when talking about her Cecilia? She had been three years older than Sammy, and they had adored each other. And now she was gone, but he could talk about her as if he'd seen her only yesterday. She sighed.

As she scrubbed the brush over teeth, she let her mind drift back to the forest . . .

Caritas sat tall in her saddle, facing Mort, her eyes mockingly triumphant.

He glared at her. He was unaccustomed to being thwarted, especially by a young girl.

"Tie her hands," he growled at one of his minions. "She won't need them, since she's such a good rider." Turning to Caritas, he snarled, "Your brothers may have escaped me for now, but we will find them. And I still have you. Your uncle will still pay a hefty bounty for his brother's oldest child."

Caritas gasped. "Uncle Frederick? He put you up to this? Why?" she gasped in disbelief.

Mort snickered, "Can't you guess? Not so clever after all, are you my lady? As the reigning king's younger brother, he was in line for the throne. Unfortunately the king produced heirs of his own. If all of you were out of the way, he would once again be the heir apparent. Though why he should bother about you, I cannot fathom."

Caritas's back stiffened. Though she was the oldest child, the throne fell to the next male heir. She could only inherit if there were no other heirs. And even then, she would have to have a husband to fill the place of the king in wartime and in the king's judicial capacity . . . So, why indeed should her uncle be so interested in her being removed? The boys were the only threat to his plan. Maybe Caritas had not been so clever after all.

Carrie started as she felt Sammy tug on her leg. She remembered her promise to her mother and forced herself to be present to Sammy.

"Let's go down for breakfast," she said as she took Sammy by the hand.

Carrie's mind was whirling as she served Sammy his food from the hotel buffet. She put a muffin and a banana on a plate and filled a glass with milk. The familiar tightness rose up in her chest as she thought of Cecilia. After she settled Sammy down at one of the small tables she went to get her own breakfast. Sitting across from Sammy, she began to wonder about what he had told her. Was it possible that he had really seen Cecilia? Or had he just dreamed about her? Or was it just that he missed his playmate? She shook her head angrily. Of course it was a dream. It had to be. Cecilia was gone.

"You okay?" Sammy asked, regarding her solemnly over his muffin. He reached one of his hands across the table and patted hers affectionately.

"Yeah." She hated being abrupt with him, but she couldn't find another way to respond. Why did it have to be like this? Would it always be this way?

Jonny dropped into a chair next to Sammy, somehow able to juggle a bowl of cereal, a plate of pastries, and a tall glass of juice. Instead of attacking his food, though, he paused when he saw her expression. His brow furrowed exactly the way their father's did when he was concerned.

"You okay?" he asked, unwittingly echoing his baby brother's question.

That only irritated Carrie further. "Sammy dreamed about Cecilia last night," she answered in frustration.

"Oh," Jonny said, with a look of surprise and sadness.

Somehow even Jonny's sadness seemed different than her deep ache.

"No," Sammy said firmly.

Carrie and Jonny looked at him.

"What?" Now it was Carrie's turn to be surprised.

"I didn't dream. I saw her. Silly came and talked to me," Sammy spoke with all the assurance a three-year-old could muster while attempting to peel a banana.

"Sammy, that's not possible. Silly's gone." Carrie tried to be as gentle as possible. But she didn't want him to believe his sister was coming back.

"But Silly talked to me!" Now the stubborn set of his chin was unmistakable.

Carrie gave in. "Okay, fine. Whatever." She didn't want a scene right now, anyway.

"Hey, are you guys almost done?" a cheerful voice asked. Her dad had approached their table unobserved. When he sensed the tension between Carrie and Sammy, his tone changed. "Are you guys all right?" he asked while adjusting his thick glasses and looking at them with concern.

"We're fine. I'm done." Carrie dumped her half-finished breakfast in the trash.

Mr. Adams realized they weren't fighting and smiled at her. "Can you help me load up? Jonny, can you bring Sammy back to the room when he's finished?"

"Sure," Carrie and Jonny answered at the same time.

"Thanks," he said, ruffling Carrie's hair affectionately. He'd done this since she was little, but lately it annoyed her.

Sammy continued to tackle his banana, and Carrie followed her father back to the room. She grabbed a few duffle bags and went out to the van. She dumped them in the trunk and then sat on the bumper. She fingered her locket and half-closed her eyes . . .

Chapter 3

❦

*T*he remaining men in Caritas's retinue were disarmed
and roped together. They were forced to march on foot
as armed guards rode beside them.

"If you dare set a foot out of line," said Mort threaten-
ingly, "I will not hesitate to put an arrow through any of your
men."

Caritas disdained to answer, though her heart sank
with fear. There was no other threat that would have held any
weight with her, and Mort knew it.

"Don't listen to him, my lady!" a young soldier shouted
from the ranks of the prisoners. He was harshly silenced by a
kick to the head from one of the mounted guards. The young
soldier reeled from the blow, and Caritas lurched forward
with a cry. The soldier, however, regained his footing and
smiled at the princess, though his lip was bleeding.

Caritas glared at Mort and yelled, "How dare you!
Your quarrel is with me and my family. Since when has abus-
ing prisoners been written into the warrior's code?"

"Warrior's code, girl?" Mort laughed, leaning far back

in his saddle. "Mercenaries have no code but to deliver the goods for which they have been paid. If it means I have to crack a few skulls to keep you in line, then so be it. You just keep your dainty little fingers out of trouble, and no harm will come to you or to your men. Otherwise, their safety is by no means guaranteed. I wasn't paid to deliver them alive."

Caritas turned from him in disgust, touching her locket for comfort. His behavior was completely logical and totally brutal. How could she prevail against such odds?

"Carrie?"

Carrie opened her eyes to find her father gazing at her with a troubled look. He leaned against the bumper beside her and half-heartedly ruffled her hair.

"Are you really all right?" he asked with concern. "You seem to be having a very hard time lately."

Though Mr. Adams was a talented professor of ancient history, he was not always the best at putting his thoughts into words. *Especially lately,* Carrie thought. As she looked up to answer, however, she noticed the depth of worry behind his simple question.

"Yeah, I'm having a hard time. It's just a lot all at once. Cecilia, moving, losing all my friends," she responded, trying to keep the bitter edge out of her voice. The move was because of her father's job, after all. That made him mostly responsible for all of her problems in the first place.

He hesitantly put his arm around her shoulders.

"Carrie, I'm sorry. I know this is hard on you, more so than on your brothers. But I really believe it's the best decision for our family. It's a small miracle that I was offered a job there at all. I'll finally be teaching at a Catholic college and the salary is better. This is the path God is offering us. If you try to see it that way, maybe it will be a little easier to bear," he encouraged.

He let go of her shoulder and stepped around so that he was facing her. When she met his eyes, the care and worry were still there, but there was also a sparkle of humor. Their personalities were very much alike and they both knew it.

"You're a strong girl, Carrie. I know we can make this work. It's not going to be easy, but you can choose to try to accept this change. We can't make that choice for you, but we're here to talk about it and help you if you want," he said.

"Okay," Carrie muttered, shrugging. She really didn't want to have this conversation, even though she knew in her heart that what he was saying was true. Maybe she wasn't giving it a fair chance. But it was much easier not to try.

Her father sighed and smiled. He could see the familiar signs of stubbornness. Both Sammy and Carrie could dig in their heels when they had a mind to.

"Well, we'd better go. Let's collect your brothers," he said.

Carrie shrugged again and followed him back to the hotel room.

Once they were all in the van, Carrie grabbed her backpack and sat back, hardly noticing as they pulled out of the parking lot. Her ankle knocked against one of the plastic tubs of school books carefully wedged under the seats. It was almost the end of August and they would start the school year shortly after arriving in Green Bay, continuing to homeschool as they had done Carrie's whole life. Carrie groaned to herself. On top of everything else, math classes were looming inevitably in her near future.

Sighing, she yanked her bag onto her lap and reached in for a book. There had to be something she could escape into: *The Fellowship of the Ring*; *Emma*; *Mara, Daughter of the Nile*; *The Silver Branch*. All her familiar, beloved favorites, like old friends. And she had a few new ones: *The Ballad of the White Horse*, *The Silmarillion*, and *A Bear Called Paddington*. *That last one would be for reading to Sammy*, she decided. Vaguely irritated that she hadn't packed any of the Horatio Hornblower books that Meg had recommended the last time she had seen her friend, she picked up *The Ballad of the White Horse*, hoping to lose herself in the language.

As the miles raced under the car, she made her way through the puzzling introduction. Then she was swept away by the rhythm and beauty of the story of a fallen king. The words wrapped around her mind like a comforting blanket. The anguish of the conquered king spoke to her aching heart, and the tale of the resurrection of the English army and the fall of the Danes set her blood thumping.

Caritas sat up straight against the pole stuck in the ground to which she was tied, her hands tightly fastened behind her. She couldn't move. No one had bothered to gag her. Caritas was too proud to indulge in useless screaming, and no one would hear her anyway.

Though her body was bound, her mind worked furiously. How could she escape without endangering the lives of her servants and soldiers? She would certainly be missed before she could help them escape. Mort had made very clear what would happen to them if she didn't cooperate. Her brow furrowed in an expression of disgust and anger. What could she do, all on her own?

Unexpectedly, from the darkness behind her, she felt a hand covering her mouth. She tried to cry out, but the hand stifled the sound.

"Shhh, Your Highness!" a vaguely familiar voice whispered.

"If I uncover your mouth, will you promise to be quiet?" the voice, low and urgent, hissed again.

She nodded her assent.

The hand was removed cautiously, but remained ready to stop a cry if necessary. Caritas was silent, as she promised.

She felt herself being cut free and she sprang to her feet. She peered into the shadows, looking for the owner of the low voice and helpful hands. She could see a shape in the shadows beckoning her urgently.

She shook her head. "I can't go. Mort will kill the others."

"Don't worry. They're already well taken care of. Come with me. Now!"

Accustomed to giving rather than taking orders, Caritas's back stiffened. Then she paused, glancing toward the camp bonfire, where Mort and his men were celebrating their success. She hesitated for a moment. Which would it be: the devil she knew, or the danger she didn't?

She sprinted into the shadows after her liberator.

Before her eyes could adjust to the darkness, a hand grasped her wrist and led her firmly and surely away from the camp behind them.

When they finally reached a clearing, the moonlight gave everything an eerie monochromatic look. Caritas could now get a look at her rescuer. She saw a handsome, adolescent face. She also noticed his swollen lower lip.

"You!" Caritas exclaimed. "You're the soldier they kicked for speaking to me."

He grinned, clearly pleased to have been remembered.

"I am indeed. I just wanted you to know that you might have been captured but you weren't defeated. Your hand-picked retinue was ready for anything Mort's men could throw at us," he said proudly.

"By getting beaten up?" she asked sarcastically. "Well, I thank you. But are you certain the others are going to be all right?"

"Certain sure," he said. "The men dispersed even before I came and released you. We were prepared for such an attack. Remember the few men who bolted when we were ambushed? One man left to ride straight back to your parents at top speed. He won't sleep till he gets there. One rode straight on to your aunt's palace, where we were originally bound. One doubled back and untied us. And we did the rest. All the men have gone off in pairs, some on horseback, some on foot. And the best part is Mort and his scum won't know which pair you're with. So he will either spend hours following separate trails or he's going to end up empty-handed. I made sure we crossed tracks with at least two other pairs of men. You're safe, Your Highness."

Caritas was amazed by the ingenuity and simplicity of the escape.

"Again, I thank you. May I know my rescuer's name?" she asked.

"Roan, Your Highness, at your service," he responded.

"Please, call me Caritas," she insisted.

Roan grinned again as he declined. "Thank you, Your

Highness, but my father would have my head for that. Now we must press on. Follow me then."
And they set off into the woods.

Carrie's head jerked up. She realized she had gone from her book to her daydream world to dozing off. The van was pulling into the parking lot of a rest stop for lunch. After some sandwiches and fruit, they were back on the road. Carrie ticked off the days on her fingers: two days down. Another one in progress. At least one more to go before they reached Green Bay.

Carrie still didn't feel like reading, and she was growing tired of listening to the same music. She shoved her hands into the pocket of her jeans and her fingers reached her rosary beads. She pulled them out and held them. Their familiar weight in her hand gave her a tiny bit of comfort.

"Hey!" called Jonny. He lobbed a crumpled piece of paper at her to make sure he had her attention.

Carrie glanced at him with irritation. He grinned and crossed his eyes.

"What?" she asked sharply.

He grinned and asked, "Wanna play my game?" He waved his handheld video game in her direction.

Her expression softened. "No, thanks. I'm all right."

"Okay. Just asking," he said, sounding disappointed. He was about to say something else, but stopped and went back to his game.

Just then Sammy woke from a nap. He was cranky, which wasn't like him. Carrie wondered if he also felt how much life was changing for them. Mom tried to comfort him from the front seat. It wasn't working. He began to wail and couldn't be quieted. The noise became exasperating to Carrie and she closed her eyes to escape.

Caritas stumbled in the dark after Roan. The boy must have eyes like a cat, she thought. While she was clumsy and disoriented, Roan seemed to know every rock and tree in the woods. He found sure footing and a silent path while Caritas slipped noisily after him. Inwardly she fumed with indignation at his inattentiveness to her, but, remembering the gratitude she owed him, she kept silent. Finally they approached another clearing.

As Caritas took in the surroundings she realized they were not alone. Suddenly a burly figure stood up and approached them.

"It's about time, boy," a familiar voice growled, "and Her Highness looks fair spent."

"Ryan!" Caritas cried.

Another, much smaller figure sat up. "Caritas?" Jonathon's sleepy voice mumbled. Caritas assumed the small figure lying next to him was a sleeping Samuel.

"Shhh, sleep now, lad. Your sister's in safe hands," Ryan assured the boy.

Jonathon mumbled something and rolled over in his blanket.

Caritas threw her arms around Ryan, taking him off guard for once. He awkwardly patted her shoulder. Roan stood at attention, chest puffed out, grinning.

"Ryan, Roan was magnificent! He freed everyone and then led me through the dark right to you! He deserves a medal for bravery."

Roan's grin widened. Then he said sarcastically, "Save your breath, Your Highness. The best I'll get out of that old codger is a stern nod for services rendered."

Ryan dismissed the remark with a grunt. Puzzled, Caritas looked from one to the other.

"But," she began hesitantly, "you were marvelous. I don't understand . . . ."

"The old man believes praise makes a man soft. If he simply ignores my effort, I'll try harder. Isn't that right?" Roan asked, facing the hardened soldier.

Caritas wondered at the young man's flippant tone with his superior officer. She continued to look questioningly at the two men.

Ryan grumbled something that might have been "Good work."

Roan laughed aloud. "You see? He's always pushing me harder. Well, I suppose that is natural since I'm his son," Roan added.

Caritas felt her jaw drop.

"No need for that, boy," growled the surly old guard.

Caritas gasped, "You never told me you had a son!"

Ryan shrugged, "My lady, you never asked."

Now Caritas turned to the boy to ask, "And you are a guard, like your father?"

Roan agreed with a laugh, "Well, yes, for now I am. Someday I'll be a better guard than my father."

Ryan snorted and extended his hand to his son, who clasped it eagerly in a gesture of profound affection.

Caritas studied the two more closely. They were fleeing a formidable enemy through a strange forest with very valuable cargo in tow. The risks were great. Though the boy seemed arrogant and offhand and the older man disgruntled and detached, she suspected that they were deeply happy to see each other again.

Roan was the first to break the silence, "So, old man, where to now?"

Chapter 4

After one more long day of standard hotel rooms, standard hotel breakfasts, and long hours in their van, the family had almost reached Green Bay.

Carrie settled herself into her seat after their last stop for gas, fumbling in her pocket for her earbuds, which seemed hopelessly tangled with her rosary.

"So," Jonny said eagerly, "there's going to be lots of snow in Wisconsin, not like home in Washington. That's going to be so amazing! I can't wait to go sledding."

Carrie shook her head, saying, "No snow till November, probably. Don't break out your mittens just yet. It's going to be warm there right now."

"Um, Carrie," he began hesitantly at first, then in one hurried breath, "where do you go, when you're, you know, off in space? I mean, your eyes are closed, but I know you're not sleeping. And sometimes I hear you saying something, but you're not talking to us."

Carrie sighed. How could she explain this to anyone?

"I just . . . tell myself a story. Pretend I'm someone else for a while. It's . . . easier than being me, you know?"

Jonny nodded sadly, "I guess. That bad, huh?"

"Well, what do you think?" Carrie snapped, suddenly losing her temper. "No home, no friends, no sister. How much worse can it be?"

Mrs. Adams turned around and warned, "That's enough, you two."

Jonny bit his lip and looked away. Carrie could see she had hurt him.

"Jonny, I'm sorry, I just . . ." She couldn't find the right words.

"No, it's okay," he said as he looked out the window. "I just don't like to see you so . . . alone, I guess."

Carrie sighed, "I know. I'm just . . . just hurting and it's easier to be alone."

"Okay," Jonny nodded with understanding, "just wanted to let you know I'm still here." He turned to look out his window again.

Carrie smiled a little. Classic Jonny. Easygoing. Refusing to hold a grudge. Sometimes she wondered what went on under that calm surface.

He had to miss Cecilia too. She wondered what it was like to be so easygoing. She sighed and deliberately closed her eyes.

"So, old man, where to now?" Roan questioned his father.

"Now we get the princess and her brothers to safety. We will continue on course for their aunt's palace as before the ambush. Mort will likely expect us to flee back to their home. So he won't keep as thorough a watch on the western road as on the eastern. I am certain their aunt, Lady Joan, will send a mounted guard to find and escort us once she hears of the ambush. We'll make our way on foot till then."

"But now that I know that Frederick is plotting against my family," Caritas objected, "I must go back. I must warn them."

Ryan shook his head, and reasoned, "That's exactly what Frederick would want you to do, my lady. You would only put yourself in graver danger by being within his reach. The safest thing to do is to go forward, to Lady Joan's palace. We can protect you there."

"But I can save the others by telling them who their enemy is! Don't you understand?" she questioned desperately.

"My lady, don't underestimate your parents. They may already know about your Uncle Frederick. It doesn't take a genius to figure out who would inherit the throne if the king and his family were out of the way."

Caritas paused in her mounting tirade to ask, "Ryan,

why did Frederick want Mort to capture me? Of what use am I?"

Roan coughed to catch their attention. Ryan glanced at him and nodded.

Roan continued, "Well, for one thing, Your Highness, you obviously make a valuable hostage. With you as a bargaining chip your uncle could force your parents to do any number of things. And technically," he paused and looked embarrassed, "technically Your Highness can inherit, under . . . certain conditions."

"But how would that help Frederick . . . ?" Caritas's voice trailed off, still filled with confusion.

Roan answered, "The conditions, Your Highness, would include marriage. My guess would be that Frederick doesn't intend to marry you himself. No, he would probably marry you to Claude, the son he keeps tightly under his thumb. Then Frederick would still be, in effect, the reigning monarch. Pretty devious, eh?"

Caritas nodded. It all made sense.

"We've got to stop him. People have to see what he's doing. I've got to go back!" she insisted.

Ryan disagreed again, saying, "And throw yourself right into his arms? No, you are coming with us to Lady Joan's palace. There you will be safe and out of Frederick's reach. Do you understand me?"

Caritas glowered at him for his refusal, but she knew he had a point. She nodded her reluctant assent. For now, it was probably the wisest choice. She could make other plans later, when her brothers were safe.

With their course of action set, the adrenaline that had sustained Caritas during the night flight began to wear off. Fatigue left her limbs and eyes heavy. She needed rest.

Ryan's gruff face softened as he recognized her exhaustion. He took a spare cloak from his pack and slung it around the weary girl's shoulders, leading her to her brothers. She lay down an arm's length from Samuel, whose face was peaceful in sleep. As she drifted off, she heard Ryan speaking in a low voice to his son.

"I'll take first watch, boy. You get some rest," the older man said. Then, awkwardly, he added, "You did well tonight, son. I would have trusted her to no one else. I know you will help me to keep her safe."

"Of course, father," Roan replied.

"Carrie! We're here!" Her mother's voice jerked Carrie out of the forest. They had arrived.

Chapter 5

Two hours after their arrival in Green Bay, Carrie lay in her sleeping bag, staring at the ceiling of their hotel room. A breeze drifted in from an open window. The weather was calm, even pleasant, just like the rest of her family. There would have to be rolling thunder and lightening or maybe an earthquake for nature to express how she was feeling. She blinked back her tears. She set her jaw, determined not to feel sorry for herself. It didn't work. She felt *very* sorry for herself. She felt somehow that nothing would ever work out for her, ever again. Her world was falling apart. *Where is God?* She rolled over on to her stomach and curled her rosary around her hand, clutching it for the sheer physical reassurance it gave her.

Then she almost screamed when she felt a hand on her head.

"Sammy! You scared me," she said with relief. "What's wrong?"

"Carrie," Sammy whispered, "can I sleep by you tonight? I'm lonely." His warm, slightly sticky hand touched her face. Carrie reached over and brought Sammy's little body next to hers. She draped an arm around him and he snuggled closer.

"Sammy, why are you lonely?" she asked quietly.

"Jonny's sleeping. And everything's different again," he whimpered. There was something in his voice Carrie didn't often hear from her willful brother. She squeezed him in a hug.

"It's okay, Sammy, I'm here," she reassured him.

"I know," Sammy sighed contentedly.

Carrie felt his body gradually relaxing into sleep under her arm. Suddenly, the world didn't seem so lonely anymore. Her mind wandered back to her story as she waited for sleep to come.

Morning gently reached the clearing, waking Caritas with a beam of golden light.

She yawned and sat up, looking around her. She wondered for a moment where everyone was. Then the events of the night before came flooding back, and she glanced anxiously around. Both her brothers were there, sleeping soundly, and Ryan was lying a bit further off. Roan was the only one awake. He grinned and tossed her an apple he pulled from his pack. She was about to speak when Roan placed a finger over his lips, indicating those still asleep with a motion of his head. She smiled and nodded.

Taking another apple from his pack, Roan walked over and sat across from Caritas.

"So, what happens today?" she whispered.

"Father believes that Lady Joan will send a guard out to meet us, so we need to steer clear of Mort till we rendezvous with them. If he's right, we'll be able to get you all to safety quickly. We were less than a day away from Lady Joan's palace when we were ambushed. If the messenger reached her last night, she probably sent a guard out immediately. If they rode through the night, we'll probably see them sometime this evening."

Caritas nodded thoughtfully. If she were careful, she would then be able to follow through with her own plans after her brothers were safely in the custody of Ryan and Lady Joan's guard. She cocked her head at Roan.

"Roan," she asked, "why did Ryan not tell me of the plans in the event of an attack? Should I not have known what to expect?"

Roan squirmed and did not meet her gaze.

"Well, Your Highness," he answered, "my father was very clear in his orders to all the men that none of us should speak of it. He believed that if you knew, you might try to override his orders. He wanted to avoid confusion."

Caritas frowned.

"If you didn't know about the plan, you couldn't forbid it," continued Roan. "And he was confident that after you'd thought about it, you'd agree."

Caritas glanced down at her hands.

"I'm sorry to have kept you in the dark, but it was for your own good. Besides, would you have listened to a humble soldier?" Now Roan was grinning at her, perhaps hoping to charm her into a smile.

Reluctantly, Caritas did smile and agree, "Ryan was probably right. It was a great risk to you all. I don't know how to thank you." Unexpectedly, she laughed and said, "That old schemer! The whole time that I was telling him of my brilliant plan to keep my brothers safe in case we were captured, he was turning around and giving other orders to keep me safe in spite of myself."

Roan smiled sympathetically. "You can't do everything yourself, Your Highness," he counseled, "and you must give my father credit. Sometimes you have to remember that there are times when someone else may know better than you. The old man's plan worked, didn't it?"

Carrie's eyes snapped open. Where had that come from? Roan was supposed to tell Caritas how brave and clever *she* was, not how brave and clever someone else was. Then she paused. *Could Roan have been right? Did it apply to her now, too?* Carrie quickly pushed that thought aside. She wasn't interested in her story anymore just then.

Very early the next morning Carrie woke up disoriented. Her heart was racing and she was gasping for air. She sat up and looked around. Sammy was still sleeping peacefully beside her. She shook her head to clear it of her uneasy sleep and her frightening dream. Her nightmare. That was it. She drew a long, shuddering breath as she tried to remember what had scared her awake. There had been a jumble of faces, and she was trying to run with a child in her arms. *Cecilia.* She had been trying to rescue Cecilia from something. Carrie dropped back onto her pillow, refusing to recall any further. She sighed, stared at the ceiling, and conjured up instead Roan's smiling face.

The two men, the two boys, and the girl trudged through the woods. The men made almost no noise. The children were not quite as deft, but they learned quickly, in part because of Ryan's skillful instruction, in part because they feared that every rustle of leaves might signal possible danger. They feared mercenaries in every shadow and arrows in the swish of every squirrel's tail.

Three times that day the five travelers halted, hiding in convenient trees or hollows, waiting for the sounds of pursuit to die away. Once they even caught a glimpse of a few of Mort's mercenaries. From the grumbling exchange they overheard, Mort had been furious over the captives' escape and every last one of his men had paid for it dearly. Caritas smiled as she crouched in her hiding place, clutching her locket.

After hours of hiking through the ancient forest, Ryan silently called a halt by raising his arm above his head.

Jonathan and Samuel froze, fearing that more troops were approaching. They stood a mere stone's throw from the road. Soon they could all hear the thud of hooves and the chink of harnesses. Ryan looked at Roan, who crept silently toward the dangerous thoroughfare.

Within minutes they heard many voices. Fearing the worst, Caritas turned in anguish to her bodyguard, sure that his face would reflect her despair. Instead, the soldier wore a satisfied smile.

"Come," he told his charges, "Lady Joan's search party has arrived."

The children emerged onto the wide road, blinking in the late afternoon sunlight. Catching sight of the small party, the men hailed them with hearty cheers. The small army, wearing Lady Joan's livery of green and silver, dismounted. Caritas watched Roan chatting animatedly with some of the men, his gold and red clothing standing out from the rest.

As the initial joy died down, Caritas heard a woman's voice issuing orders. Before she had a chance to place it, she was enveloped in a strong pair of arms. Her cousin Lady Maybelle exclaimed, "Caritas, my little one, we were so worried about you! Thank goodness we found you before those cutthroats did!"

Lady Maybelle released her cousin and held her at arm's length. "From now on, young lady," she said firmly, "you will not be out of my sight till Mother's walls are between you and those brigands. Oh, Caritas, I'm so glad you're safe." Lady Maybelle hugged her again.

Carrie fell back asleep embraced by a sense of being comforted.

Chapter 6

The next day, Carrie's father left to fly back to Washington to supervise the moving of their furniture and other belongings. The plan was for Mr. Adams to return to Green Bay within the week. Carrie, Jonny, Sammy, and Mrs. Adams would stay at the hotel for the week, making local connections and beginning the process of house-hunting. Their mother had the phone numbers of a few local families with distant ties to other home-schoolers in Washington. Through them she had found a reputable realtor, who was now helping them find a place to live.

Before he left, Mr. Adams spoke with each of his children privately. Carrie was last. His face re-laxed into his familiar smile when he saw her. Car-rie thought she saw a glint of pride in his brown eyes, but she couldn't be sure.

"Carrie," he began earnestly, "I need you to help your mother while I'm gone. I know you'll pitch in till I get back. I don't need to tell you how important this is to everyone. Sammy will probably be a bit difficult, but he's little, and in some ways this move has been harder on him than on anyone else. Jonny will listen to you, so please be a good influence on him."

Carrie nodded at the stream of instructions. She was glad and proud that her father trusted her. For the first time, she felt like she was being treated like an adult. Unconsciously, she straightened her posture.

Her father picked up a plastic grocery bag from the floor.

"I know this is going to be a long week for everyone," he said. "So I have a few things to help you pass the time."

He handed her the bag. Inside was the book *Silas Marner* by George Elliot, an author Carrie hadn't heard of before. There were also some pastels with a new sketch pad. Carrie hugged her father, and he wrapped one arm around her and held her head to his chest for a moment. Then he kissed the top of her head and let her go.

"Thanks, Dad. These are wonderful," she said.

When her father left, Carrie looked at her gifts. She was touched by her dad's attention. New books were always a treat. The pastels were clearly to encourage her sketching, a pastime she enjoyed and one that made her father proud. When she showed her brothers her gifts, she found out that Jonny had gotten a new game for his game console and Sammy had gotten some building blocks and crayons.

To help pass the long days, Mrs. Adams had brought all their school books. Carrie was in eighth grade, on the brink of high school. Jonny was starting sixth grade. Sammy was just beginning to learn his letters and numbers, and he could already write his name.

Later that day, Carrie groaned as she cracked open her new math book. Math was the worst of her subjects —she was much better at subjects with some room for creativity. She mulled over the review lessons, feeling something between frustration and boredom. She glanced around the room. Jonny was bent over an English book. Mom was helping Sammy with the letter "G." Furtively, Carrie relaxed slightly and closed her eyes.

Caritas was grateful for the guard and even more grateful for Lady Joan and Lady Maybelle's thoughtfulness. Clean changes of clothes, fresh food, warm blankets. They seemed to have prepared for a long journey—longer than the day and a half needed to reach the palace. Lady Maybelle supervised Jonathan and Samuel while Caritas became acquainted with her new mount, Brownie, a frisky bay mare. Caritas won the horse over immediately when she slipped her an apple. Caritas also personally saddled and adjusted the harness and trappings on the beautiful horse. And, when no one was looking, she also started loading her saddlebags. She made sure she had enough provisions for at least a week, as well as a knife and a flint and steel set.

Everyone's attention was focused on preparing for the journey. Ryan was supervising the packing of the mounts for the boys. Lady Maybelle was double-checking the supply ponies, and most of the soldiers were listening to a tale being told by a commanding officer. Only Roan appeared impatient to be on the way, already atop his mount.

Caritas seized the chance. She mounted, wheeled Brownie around to face the direction from which they had come, and dug her heels hard into the mare's sides. Brownie reared and then bolted. Away from the palace, away from safety—toward Caritas's parents who needed her. She felt the wind rush through her hair and with it the exhilaration of success. Her plan had worked.

In the clearing there were shouts of alarm mingled with commands.

"Roan!" Ryan shouted at his son. "Go!"

Roan plunged into a headlong chase of the princess.

Caritas, realizing she was being pursued, urged Brownie to still greater efforts.

Carrie opened her eyes and sighed, looking out the window into the hotel parking lot. She dug back into her algebra. If only her life could be more like Caritas's . . .

Chapter 7

The days passed quickly as the family waited for Mr. Adams to return. Carrie sensed her mother was keeping them busy with school work to prevent them from going stir-crazy in the small hotel room.

At first, Mrs. Adams also made sure the children made daily trips to explore their new town. They visited various grocery stores, walked through the mall, and saw several beautiful parks and neighborhoods. After the fourth day, however, Carrie could see her mother's exhaustion. Carrie took Jonny aside and talked to him about it. Together they confronted their mother. They told her that they would take Sammy on short walks around the hotel for exercise. Carrie could see that her mother was surprised but pleased that her two oldest children had noticed and taken initiative. She agreed. Carrie smiled in satisfaction, feeling she was living up to her father's expectations.

After that, their only "field trip" for the week was Mass, which they attended at the diocesan cathedral. The church, larger than any Carrie had seen in Washington, was breathtakingly beautiful to Carrie, who loved the paintings and stained glass windows.

Later that day, Carrie checked her email on the family laptop and found a message from Meg! She clicked on it and read eagerly. The email began with Meg's typical greeting, and Carrie could almost hear Meg's chirpy voice.

Hiya, girl!

It's been raining here a lot, but that's not a surprise. I can't believe you're gone. It doesn't even seem real to me. I saw Brent at the home-school picnic last weekend. He's so hot. Can you believe, he actually asked about you? By name! I told him what happened and he seemed disappointed. I guess he hadn't heard, since they do live like way out in Seattle, but still! Do you want me to give him your email address? Maybe he'll write to you! Anyway, thanks so much for being the reason he talked to me. It totally made my heart skip a beat! What are you reading now? I'm reading the second Horatio Hornblower book. Even though it starts off kind of awkwardly, it's easy to see why they used to be so popular. I bet he looks just like Brent. Well, at least he does in my head!

Miss you lots. You seriously need to move back here the minute you turn eighteen.

Hugs,
Meg

Carrie's mind was spinning. She quickly tapped out a reply without really thinking about what she was writing. Not only did Meg miss her, which was comforting, but Brent missed her, too! Or at least he had noticed she was gone. She sighed. She knew exactly what Meg meant by her heart skipping a beat. Carrie's had skipped every time she saw him. That didn't happen very often, but usually they went to the same church, St. Augustine Parish, so it had been almost once a week.

She signed off her account and grabbed her backpack. She then crept into a corner of the room where she had some privacy. Carrie rummaged through her collection of books and picked up *The Ballad of the White Horse* again. She flipped it open to where she had left off: the Virgin Mary had just appeared to Alfred. Carrie was really excited about the apparition. *Was Mary going to give Alfred a weapon? A secret to defeating the horrible Danes? Her blessing?* As Carrie's mind soaked in the story, she began to feel confused. The apparition didn't seem to have anything to do with Alfred. Instead, the Virgin promised only that things were going to get worse. *What?* Carrie snapped the book shut in annoyance.

Now she couldn't shake the feeling that everyone was out to get her today. Even Chesterton's beautiful poetry. Not fair. She clutched her locket, fighting to hold back a wave of pain. Maybe Meg was right. Maybe she should go back to Washington. But how could she wait until she was eighteen? Could she live with the ache in her heart that long?

Tree branches whipped past her face as Caritas urged Brownie forward. She would not be caught and dragged back. Not only would she have failed in her attempt to warn her parents, but the thought of the humiliation of being escorted back like a naughty child was more than she could bear.

As good a mount as Brownie was, the saddlebags Caritas had packed hung heavy and slowed the horse down. Caritas felt the horse's flanks heaving. Unwilling to injure the mare, and resigning herself to the inevitable, Caritas slowed the horse down to a canter. Like an arrow from a bow, Roan sped through the underbrush and wheeled his horse around to intercept Caritas's. Her heart shuddered when she saw the stormy expression on his face, but outwardly she sat straight and haughty in the saddle.

"What is wrong with you?" Roan yelled, disregarding

the fact that she was a princess. "Do you want to be captured? Should I just escort you back to Mort's men?"

Caritas had never seen anyone so angry at her before. Part of her wanted to melt into tears, but she refused to.

"Might I remind you, soldier, that you are addressing the firstborn of the royal family? I am fully capable of taking care of my own person and will thank you not to interfere with my plans," she retorted with cold aristocratic politeness. Then, seeing a change in Roan's expression, she almost pleaded, "Roan, my parents are in danger. I might be able to help them. If you knew your father was in danger of being harmed by an enemy, wouldn't you hurry to warn him?"

Roan grew visibly calmer, but he continued to reprove her, saying, "There is a vast difference between the two situations. I would at least stand some chance of helping him if he were in danger. And I could not be used as a pawn in a larger game. What you're doing is madness. Frederick is playing a deadly game of chess, and your actions might enable him to capture the queen. Then, no matter how great the danger to your parents is now, you would have made the situation infinitely worse. Do you want your parents to be forced to choose between the throne and your life? Or to watch as you wed against your will to satisfy your uncle's ambition?"

Caritas swallowed hard in an effort not to hard in an effort not to cry. "Roan, I know it seems unreasonable and foolish, but I have to warn my parents. I'll be careful, I promise. I have to try to save them!" She stopped speaking as her voice cracked with emotion.

Roan's face softened. "Your Highness," he said, "I understand that you love your parents and that you want to see them safe. But believe me, they want your safety above all else. Will you please accompany me back to Lady Maybelle's retinue?"

Caritas looked him straight in the eye and said firmly, "No, Roan, I cannot do that. Please convey my regrets and let them know I will join them after delivering the warning to my parents."

Roan shook his head in half-resignation and said, "Your Highness, if you think for a moment that I'm going back to my father empty-handed, you really are mad." He smiled grimly. "No, I am now your travel companion and faithful body guard. If Mort does capture you, it will be over my dead body."

Caritas smiled back at her loyal bodyguard. "Thank you, Roan. I'll find some way to pay you back, I swear."

"Never mind," he responded, somewhat ungraciously. "If we make it through this journey alive, that will be reward enough."

Chapter 8

After a week away, Mr. Adams returned to Green Bay in a loaded rental truck. He looked tired but happy to see his wife and children. He gave Sammy, Jonny, and Carrie turns riding around the hotel parking lot in the front seat of the truck. Carrie was startled by how far above the other cars they were, but she gradually began to enjoy the sensation.

The realtor had called with a list of houses for her parents to look at. Reluctantly, they left Carrie in charge of the boys. They locked the door and told her not to open it for strangers. They extracted solemn promises from the boys to behave.

The first hour went well. Jonny and Sammy watched a movie they'd already seen. After the movie, they began to play a game. Carrie had her nose buried in a book. When they began to get louder, Carrie warned them to quiet down. They paid no attention to her. Carrie sighed with exasperation. The noise was giving her a headache. She took Meg's headband off, rubbed her forehead, and put her earbuds in. As she tapped her feet to her music, the boys were getting more rowdy, but she ignored them. Suddenly her earbuds were jerked from her ears. The boys were tumbling around in blankets next to her, shouting and giggling. Then there was a terrible crunching sound—and deafening silence.

"Are you all right?" Carrie yelled. She had no idea what the sound might have been.

The boys nodded their heads slowly. They began to look through the pile of blankets. Then both boys looked up at Carrie, wide-eyed with fear. Carrie, knowing that only something *really* bad could make her brothers look so solemn, swept the blankets aside.

Her headband—Meg's headband—was on the floor in several pieces. The damage was clearly irreparable.

Carrie wanted to scream and cry. She wanted to punish her brothers for destroying something so important to her. But, seeing the fear in their eyes, she could not. She knew it was her fault anyway. If she had put the headband somewhere safe, it wouldn't have been broken.

So she quietly picked up the pieces, scowled at her brothers, and curled up in the corner. She turned her music up so loud her head throbbed. Her brothers crept off to separate corners. Carrie covered her face with her hands.

Caritas and Roan continued to bicker as they traveled further away from safety. Caritas felt certain hers was the right course of action and that she knew the fastest route through the woods. Roan disagreed on both counts.

"I beg to differ, Your Highness," Roan said with a note of sarcasm, "but the fastest way through the woods is straight south and then west. Then we would avoid the Hungry Marshes and the Robber Woods. Leave it to a woman to insist on following a course that will lead through the worst swamps in the known world, and then, if we survive that, through a forest with more brigands than trees!"

Caritas was about to retort angrily when, in the middle of the clearing they were traveling through, there stood a poorly dressed man with his arms crossed over his chest. He looked wild and unkempt, and his smile was the most unpleasant that Caritas had ever seen. Roan reigned in his horse and reached over to reign in Brownie.

"Well, children, where are you bound this fine day through these dangerous woods?" he called to them with obvious mockery in his voice.

As the man strode toward Caritas and Roan, their horses backed up nervously. Clearly, neither horse fancied the stranger's smell.

"Good day," Roan said politely. "Could you tell us the

quickest way to the road, perchance? The lady has lost her way and I was attempting to put her right."

"Well, lad, I don't rightly know the quickest way out for two children such as yourselves. Why don't you come home with me and we can ask around till you find your way?" Something in the man's voice sent a chill down Caritas's spine. She instinctively looked around.

They were surrounded. From behind the trees there emerged a dozen men with bows trained on the princess and her companion.

"Roan . . ." she began, but Roan was already aware of their situation.

"Finally!" Roan said with relief and triumph in his voice. "What took you so long?"

He dismounted to shake hands with the strangers, leaving Caritas stunned and silent. One of the outlaws took her bridle and began to lead her horse. Had she been betrayed?

Chapter 9

When Carrie's parents returned with dinner, they found Carrie curled up in the corner, facing the wall, and the boys playing quietly.

Carrie would only offer single-word answers to their questions. It was Jonny who told them about the headband.

Mrs. Adams sat down beside Carrie and stroked her hair.

"Sweetie, I'm sorry," she said. "Your brothers are sorry, too. They didn't mean to hurt you."

Carrie refused to respond.

"Carrie, I'm sure we can fix it," Mrs. Adams encouraged.

No response.

"Carrie, honey, I know you're upset, but it was just a thing. We shouldn't be so attached to things that they become more important than family."

Carrie turned to face her mother and looked

her in the eyes. "It's *not* just a 'thing,'" she snapped. "It was Meg's last gift to me. It's irreplaceable. She made it for me. I'm never going to see her again and now the last thing she ever gave me is gone!"

Though she tried to keep her voice from trembling, she couldn't hide the tears that slid down her face. So she covered her feelings with anger and hostility toward everyone in the small room. "I'd rather be back at home than here with all of you!" she shouted. "I'm never going to see home again, or my friends, or Cecilia, and it's all your fault! How could you do this to me?" Then she broke into sobs.

She ran to the bathroom—the only place where she had any privacy. There she let go her flood of tears as she rocked back and forth on the floor, trying to shut out the image of Jonny's and Sammy's terrified expressions as she shouted at them.

About fifteen minutes later, as her sobs were subsiding, her mom knocked on the door.

"Carrie, you need to come out and talk to me," she said gently. "Your father took the boys for a drive." Then with unmistakable authority and seriousness, she demanded, "Come out now."

Carrie unlocked the door and stepped out.

"Sit down, please," her mother said, indicating one of the two chairs in the room.

Carrie sat down. Her mother's voice was stern and her jaw was set in a hard line, but underneath it Carrie knew her mother was tired. Tired and sad.

Carrie quailed, realizing the pain she had caused with her angry outburst.

"Carrie, I know this move has been hard on you, and I'm sorry about that. I know your brothers should have been more careful. Your father and I will talk to them, too. But you just said some horrible things to your brothers that they did not deserve. When they get back, you are going to apologize to them. Is that understood?"

Carrie nodded guiltily.

"You should also apologize to your father," she continued. "You've been giving him the cold shoulder since we announced we were moving. This job is important to all of us, not just to him. And he misses you. You two used to be close. It's not right for you to treat him this way."

Carrie nodded again, another tear escaping.

"We all love you and we want you to be happy. However, that doesn't mean that every member of this family has to bend over backward to accommodate your moods. I'm grateful that you've tried to help more with Sammy. But you cannot hurt his feelings over an accident. If you cared so much about the headband, you should have put it somewhere safe."

Carrie looked sullen.

"Look at me, please," her mother said firmly. "We are going to make this work. We found a house today that will do temporarily. Tomorrow we'll move our things there with help from some local families I met. The day after tomorrow, we're going to a potluck for homeschoolers to begin the school year. I want you to try to make friends."

"But Mom," Carrie asserted, "I can't just produce friendships to make you happy. Meg was special. I'll never know anyone else like her." She was ashamed of her own defiance, but she could not stop herself.

"That's true, honey," Mrs. Adams agreed, "your friendship with Meg was a gift. But I know God will give you more friends here. There are many more homeschoolers in this area, so there will be plenty of people for you to meet."

Carrie looked down.

Mrs. Adams sighed and pulled her daughter close. When Carrie was younger and had thrown temper tantrums, her mother had always corrected Carrie's behavior with firmness and then held her daughter close. It had made Carrie feel safe. Now it comforted her in a way she could not express.

"Carrie, I know you think your world has come to an end," Mrs. Adams reassured her, "but you're thirteen years old. You have your whole life ahead of you. Promise me you'll try to make this work, okay?"

Carrie nodded. Did she have a choice?

Chapter 10

The next day, the whole family went to see the new house. It was a three-bedroom house on a city lot, but it had a front yard with some old maples that Jonny immediately began to climb before being called back to help unload. A few men and a boy, perhaps a year or two older than Carrie, arrived to help them unload the truck. Carrie heard the men calling the boy's name: Ben.

While everyone unloaded the moving van, Carrie watched Ben. He was pretty good-looking, and he walked with a slight limp. He was strong, well-mannered, and very helpful.

After they had finished unloading the truck and were resting inside the house, a woman and a girl walked up to the porch.

"Oh, there's Mrs. Jackson," Mom said as she went to open the front door. "We met her the other day at church, remember? She said she would come to help."

"Hello," Mrs. Jackson said cheerfully, coming into the living room from the porch. "You must be Carrie. It's good to meet you. This is my daughter, Jenny." From behind Mrs. Jackson a slim figure with big eyes and a wide, quick smile emerged.

"Hi," she said shyly.

"Hi," said Carrie awkwardly.

"Why don't you two work on unpacking here in the living room?" Mom suggested. "Mrs. Jackson and I can work in the kitchen."

Great, Carrie thought. *Alone with the new girl.*

They started opening boxes.

"So," Jenny said, "is Carrie short for something?"

"Yeah. It's Caritas." She blushed a little as she told her, wondering if Jenny would think her name was weird.

Instead Jenny smiled widely and said, "Caritas. That's pretty. It's Latin, right? I'm taking Latin this year."

Carrie nodded shyly. "My dad is kind of a geek that way. Is Jenny short for something?" *Jennifer, of course,* Carrie's mind supplied sarcastically. *What a stupid question.*

Now the other girl looked awkward. "It's Genesis, actually. My dad is kind of a geek that way, too."

Carrie impulsively felt her heart warming to

Jenny. She had never met someone with a name as unusual as her own.

"I like Genesis. It sounds cool."

Jenny smiled again. "Thanks."

There was another pause.

"So," Jenny said. "Did you move into your new room yet?"

"Well, the boxes are there, but I didn't unpack any yet," Carrie answered.

"Want help?" Jenny asked.

"Um, okay," Carrie paused, remembering how she used to share a room with Cecilia at home. "Maybe after we do this?"

"Okay," Jenny smiled.

After a late lunch of pizza and soda, Mrs. Jackson and Jenny had to leave. Ben and the other men were still helping Mr. Adams move boxes. Sammy and Jonny were playing hide-and-seek among the stacks of boxes. Carrie began wandering through the house. She opened the door to her new room. The bed frame leaned against one wall and the mattress against another. Boxes of Carrie's possessions were stacked higher than her head in a haphazard way.

With a catch in her throat, she remembered her old room, unique, slightly cluttered, filled with her things arranged just the way she wanted them. Well, almost. Sharing a room with Cecilia had forced Carrie to arrange her things so they wouldn't be damaged by a curious child. They had been good roommates. Carrie realized that her things had been packed separately from Cecilia's artwork and books and toys. The room would be just Carrie's now. The feeling of loneliness and unfamiliarity made her cry. Now, in the privacy of her own room, for the first time since moving, she slumped in a corner, next to a stack of boxes. She clutched her locket with both hands, lay her head on her knees, and sobbed.

It felt good to let it all out for once, and she felt safe knowing everyone was busy and wouldn't interrupt her.

Then she heard her door open. Her head snapped up to see Ben standing in the doorway. He stared back at her, clearly mortified.

"Oh, gosh, I'm so sorry. I thought . . . I was looking for the bathroom," he stammered, abashed and blushing furiously. "Hey," he started again, "Are you, um, are you okay?"

Carrie, wiping her sleeve across her eyes, shook her head.

Ben hesitantly came over and sat down across from her. "Do you . . . uh . . . can I . . . wanna talk about it?" he asked clumsily.

Carrie, caught off guard, suddenly let flow her tears and words without restraint.

"My baby sister died nine months ago, she was six, and we shared the same room and now we don't. And now we don't live anywhere near her and I can't visit her. And I miss her so much!" Her grief overcame her speech and she fell silent.

Ben's face registered a range of emotions, among them shock, sympathy, and embarrassment.

"Gosh, I'm so sorry. I didn't know. Is there any way . . . anything I can do?" he asked with genuine compassion.

Carrie shook her head. Ben awkwardly patted her arm. There was silence.

When Carrie could trust herself to speak again, she sniffled and looked over at Ben.

"I'm sorry. None of that is your problem. It's just been a little hard adjusting, that's all," she said.

"No, it's okay. I'm sorry I can't help," Ben responded.

Carrie smiled ruefully. "Me, too."

Ben returned her smile hesitantly, said goodbye, and left the room.

❧

After everyone had finally left, Carrie's mother began looking for her. She found Carrie in her room, wrestling with her mattress and trying to assemble her bed. Carrie had managed to put the pieces of the bed frame together and had moved it to the corner of her new room. Now she was trying, without help, to put the box spring on the frame.

"Carrie," Mrs. Adams asked, "what are you doing?"

Carrie wiped the sweat off her forehead and looked at her mother defiantly. "I'm putting my bed together. I'm tired and I don't want to sleep on the floor tonight."

Carrie's mother sighed and shook her head. "Carrie, don't you remember? We're going back to the hotel tonight. And your father would be happy to help you with that tomorrow."

"I'm doing fine," Carrie asserted stubbornly, refusing to admit that she had been trying to get the better of the box spring for the last ten minutes. She felt just a little foolish for forgetting that they wouldn't be spending the night at the house. They had, after all, left their belongings at the hotel.

Carrie's mother smiled. "Well, we're heading back to the hotel now, so how about you grab your shoes and come along? I'm sure the mattress would like a rest."

"Fine," Carrie huffed. "I'll just finish it up tomorrow."

Chapter 11

Curled up on her sleeping bag, Carrie's mind dodged from one thing to another: the new house, her old room, Cecilia, Ben, Jenny, making friends, not fitting in . . . . Her exhausted body did nothing to help her escape her active mind. She stared into the blackness of the hotel room.

Caritas could hear the raucous laughter of the outlaws in the distance. One of her feet was fastened to a tree by a fairly long rope. She could move freely within the limited confines of the rope's radius, like a leashed animal. She was furious, curled up on herself, clutching her locket as if it might give her answers.

After Roan had greeted the outlaws, he had convinced them that he had come to join them, and he offered Caritas, a "duke's daughter they could hold for a fine ransom," as a pledge of his good faith. After seeing Caritas's rich apparel and witnessing her feisty temper, the outlaws seemed inclined to believe him. And now he was drinking freely with them around their fire while she sat in the cold with a pair of sullen outlaws guarding her. *If only I could find some way to distract them,* she thought, *then I could work on the knot around my ankle.* She had already tried once, and they had threatened to tie her hands as well if she didn't behave herself.

One of the outlaws sauntered over with two mugs in one hand and a plate in the other. With a jest Caritas didn't catch, he handed the mugs to the guards and dropped the plate within her reach. After a scornful glance in his direction, she ignored him.

He seemed displeased by her attitude.

"Now, is that any way to treat your host, girl? Where I was raised, when a guest was given vittles, they were properly grateful." He moved closer to her, his stance growing threatening. "I would very much like to hear a 'thank-you' from you," he said as reached his hand toward her face.

"Nat!" The call made the man stop and turn toward his companions. "Keep your hands to yourself. Those lordly types won't pay as much for damaged goods."

Nat dropped his outstretched hand and turned, grumbling under his breath.

Caritas released a breath she hadn't realized she was holding.

As twilight deepened into nightfall, her guards were relieved by another pair. She sat huddled in her cloak, thinking feverishly, trying to figure out a way to escape. And she was angry. How could Roan have betrayed her like that?

Eventually, she heard the sound of a low, steady rumbling. She realized one of her guards was snoring. Then something dropped heavily next to her and she nearly cried out. The lithe figure put a finger to her lips.

"Hold still, Your Highness," said a familiar voice, "and I'll have you out of this knot in a moment."

Caritas felt his hand take hold of her ankle. With a steady tug he cut through the rope with a dagger. Then, with a last pull, she was free.

"Now follow me, quickly, and no more of your tricks, Your Highness, or you'll land us in hot water again."

Caritas struggled between indignation and relief as she followed Roan out of the bandits' camp. She stumbled from weariness and Roan put out a hand to steady her.

"Your Highness, I know you're tired, but we must keep moving. I drugged their ale and they will be asleep for a while, but they'll be angry as hornets when they awake. A few more miles, then we can rest."

"You drugged them?" she asked incredulously.

She could hear the amusement in Roan's voice. "Of course. How else would they have let such a hefty ransom walk away?"

"How did you know what to give them?" she asked.

"My grandmother was the best herb woman in three kingdoms. I think you'll find, Your Highness, that if you listen to those around you, you'll start hearing things more than worth your while."

Carrie drifted into a deep, exhausted sleep. The next morning she woke up groggy.

"Rise and shine," her father called out cheerily. Clearly, he was in the best of spirits, whistling through his teeth as he packed the family's remaining belongings back into duffle bags. Carrie smiled tentatively. The events of the past few days had not left them on the best of terms. He smiled back, widely and warmly. Apparently, all was forgiven.

She began to brush her hair. Thinking of her encounter with Ben made her cheeks grow hot with embarrassment. How could she have poured the pieces of her broken heart out to a boy she had just met? Perhaps it might be sweet and endearing in a romantic comedy, but in real life, it was mortifying beyond her wildest dreams.

"Sweetie, are you feeling okay?" her mother asked. Carrie jumped. She hadn't heard her mother approaching. "You look a little red," her mother continued.

"I'm okay," Carrie stammered.

Unconvinced, her mother put her hand against Carrie's forehead. "You feel a little warm. When I find the thermometer, I'm going to take your temperature."

Carrie nodded. There was no way she was going to tell her mother the reason for her hot face. She hoped no one would ever know and that Ben would wake up and think it had just been a bad dream. *Please, God,* Carrie prayed, *just let him forget. Please.* Finding her rosary in her pocket, she held it tightly for a moment of comfort.

After their final trip to the hotel's breakfast bar, the family piled into their van while Mr. Adams checked out of the hotel.

Finally, Carrie thought. They drove to their new home with the windows rolled down, enjoying the warm sun and clear skies. When they got to the house, they were in no hurry to begin the arduous process of unpacking, preferring to savor the beautiful day.

Carrie went to her room and began unpacking, putting her favorite pictures and posters up on the walls, arranging and re-arranging the furniture. No matter what she did it just didn't seem right, like a puzzle with pieces missing. As she rummaged through one of her boxes, there at the bottom she found Boo: a worn, stuffed brown bunny rabbit. It had been Cecilia's favorite toy. Looking around the room Carrie could see the gaps, places where Cecilia's things *should* have been. Choking back her tears, Carrie left to find something else to do.

Chapter 12

The following weeks were a blur of adjusting to the new house, new city, and new school work. A string of families came over with "welcome-to-the-neighborhood" meals. Carrie couldn't really keep track of their names or faces, since they came and went so quickly. Mr. Adams started his new teaching job, and every evening at supper he spoke enthusiastically about what had happened that day. When they visited the campus, it seemed nice enough to Carrie, but not so very different from the one he had taught at in Washington—expect that the campus was on a river and had a church. The little town surrounding it was also quaint, with a personality of its own.

"It feels good to settle in, finally, don't you think?" Mom commented after about a month.

"Sure," said Carrie heavily. She didn't know what the opposite of "settled" was, but whatever it was, that was how she was feeling.

But they really had settled into a routine, with the addition of many more activities and events with other homeschoolers. The homeschool group in Green Bay was large, lived closer together for the most part, and seemed to get together a lot. There were organized field trips, Friday gym days at a park, gatherings for no particular reason that Carrie could discern, and overall just a much larger social network than Carrie could have ever imagined. And that was one more change Carrie wasn't ready for.

For the first outing or two, Carrie hung back by her mother, ready to keep an eye on Sammy if her mom needed help. However, Mrs. Adams encouraged her to spend time with kids her own age. Jenny often came over to talk to Carrie. And Carrie was grateful for that. Carrie glimpsed Ben a few times, too. Once he even waved and smiled, but Carrie quickly lowered her eyes and pretended not to have noticed.

Carrie's mother learned the names of the girls Carrie's age faster than Carrie did.

"Did you hear that Kathleen's brother is entering the seminary next year?" her mother asked after one gym day.

Carrie, having no idea who Kathleen was, just shook her head.

Her mother sighed.

When she could no longer use her mother as an excuse to avoid people, Carrie started bringing a book. She would find a corner to sit in or a tree to sit under and read. After all, she didn't have the energy to socialize yet, she reasoned; she was still getting used to the changes in her life. When she was honest with herself, however, she knew she just didn't want new friends. She wanted to stop hurting. She wanted to stop losing people.

One Friday she forgot her book, so she sat under a tree and, closing her eyes, returned to her own story.

Caritas and Roan trekked cautiously through the dark forest. They had to exercise even greater vigilance to avoid being caught by Mort's men and the bandits.

By Roan's calculations, they were still some miles from the main road, which they wanted to avoid. Mort would likely still be in pursuit, and he would have spread a wide net to capture his prey.

Darkness was their one ally. They had walked all night and Caritas felt weary, but Roan continued to urge her to greater speed. The dawn would soon break and they could not lose any time.

Then, without warning, the tree line ended and they found themselves looking across a clearing. The ground was divided into precise plots full of herbs and vegetables. There were outbuildings with pens, from which they could hear the sounds of lowing and bleating. There was also a cabin with a thatched roof. Smoke curled lazily and invitingly from the chimney.

"Is it safe?" Caritas whispered to Roan.

Roan's face was serious as he considered the situation. Caritas longed to knock on the door and beg for a place by the fire. She was stiff and cold and sore.

The cabin door opened, spilling the firelight over the grass. A slight, girlish figure emerged. She was carrying a basket of greens as she walked over to one of the pens.

"Lalalalai!" she called into the pre-dawn darkness.

With a little bleat, a young she-goat emerged, leaping and turning. The girl laughed and greeted the goat cheerily, as she scratched behind its ears and fed it from her hand.

Caritas felt Roan relax.

"It's safe," he sighed.

"How do you know?" she asked breathlessly.

"She wouldn't be laughing like that if it were a trap. And the cottage and gardens are too small for a band of soldiers."

Caritas nodded in agreement.

They stepped through the tree line and began to approach the cottage. Caritas saw two shapes bounding out of the darkness before she heard the barking and growling of dogs. She turned to run back into the forest but stumbled over a tree root. She tripped and fell. Roan tried to help her up, but he could not before the dogs were upon them.

Then a clear whistle rang through the darkness, calling

the dogs to heel. The dogs backed away, but did not retreat entirely. They stood about six feet way, hair raised, growling.

Through the dim light, Caritas could see the girl approaching cautiously. She relaxed when she saw them and gave the dogs another command. With a parting snarl, the dogs trotted away.

"Good morning," the girl greeted them, as Roan helped Caritas to her feet. "What brings you to Woodhaven?"

Chapter 13

"Hey," someone said, slumping down next to Carrie.

Her eyes flew open and she found herself face to face with Ben.

"Hey," she responded warily.

"So, when are you going to come play volleyball with us?" he asked.

"I don't really play," she said guardedly.

"Well, why not?" he questioned.

"I just don't. I'm . . . not really very coordinated, so sports are kind of out for me," she fumbled through her excuse.

"First of all, I don't believe that's true. Second of all, if I can play with one bad leg, you can play with two good ones," Ben responded with exasperation.

"What?" she asked in confusion.

"When I was ten, I was in a bike accident. It tore up my shoulder and my knee. The doctors tried to fix it, but it's never been quite right since. So sports should be out for me, too, but it doesn't stop me from trying," Ben explained.

"Oh," said Carrie. "I'm sorry. I didn't know."

"Whatever," he continued impatiently. "My point is that sometimes in life, stuff changes. Stuff we don't want to change but can't control. We can let it slow us down or stop us altogether. Or we can pick ourselves up and move on."

Carrie shrugged her shoulders, trying to seem indifferent.

Ben only continued with greater determination, "Okay, it stinks to have to leave the place where you grew up and all your friends. It really stinks to lose a sister. But you can either let it ruin the rest of your life or you can start building a new one. There are so many people here who would be happy to be your friend. You're smart and interesting and pretty. So give them a chance. You might be pleasantly surprised."

Carrie sat open-mouthed and watched Ben get up.

"See you later," he said.

Carrie's mind whirled. She barely noticed Jonny coming over, until he tapped her foot with his own.

"Mom says we're leaving now," he told her.

Carrie slowly got up, her eyes still trained on

the volleyball game and her mind still reeling from what Ben had said to her.

On the way home, she couldn't think. She rubbed her forehead and stared out the window.

Caritas and Roan stood still, even after the girl called off the dogs and sent them loping back around the house. The girl put her hands on her hips and cocked her head questioningly.

Roan spoke first, "Lady, we have been traveling all night and need a place to sleep. Would you allow us to use the shelter of one of your barns? We would be on our way again by evening."

The girl's eyes narrowed as she studied the pair. "Well, you don't look like brigands, do you now?"

Caritas shuddered involuntarily. "I should hope not," she said.

"They don't travel with their women," she observed. "However, if you're trying to avoid them, you'd best tell me now."

Roan bowed as he said, "My lady, I cannot lie. We are pursued by both the brigands of the dark forest and a band of mercenaries seeking our destruction. So, on further consideration, it would be unjust to endanger you by staying here."

Caritas glanced at her companion with amusement. The courtly grace he presented to this girl was so different from the companionable, familiar tone they had begun to share.

It seemed to work, however. The girl looked pleased.

"Don't be foolish. If you are being pursued, even more reason for us to give you sanctuary. No one would look for you here. The bandits of these woods fear our dogs. And strangers learn to their cost that we are not unprotected."

The girl looked at them for a moment longer and then gestured for them to follow her, saying over her shoulder, "I will not have our guests sleeping in a barn!"

She walked carefully around the garden beds and humble stalls. She entered the front door and called out, "Grandmother, Grandfather, we have company. Come and meet our guests."

When Carrie got home, she was surprised to find another email from Meg. She hadn't heard from her in a few weeks. Her heart ached to read the message. It was Meg's usual bubbly chit-chat, but Carrie felt hurt. Apparently, life in Washington was going on . . . and without her. It seemed unfair that she should miss her friends so much while they didn't seem to miss her at all.

She went to her room and sat curled up on her bed, feeling more alone than ever.

Caritas entered a bright, cheery room with a fireplace in the center. The blaze crackled and gave off waves of heat, warming Caritas through her damp clothes. A large table with chairs around it stood in the center of the room. A man and woman, older but straight and tall, also entered the room. Caritas immediately felt at ease.

"Welcome to Woodhaven," she greeted them amiably. Her gaze moved from Roan's uniform to Caritas's tattered but rich travel dress and bright locket. She nodded to herself, as if satisfied with her thoughts. "We do not ask for names here, unless you feel like giving them. We can provide you with a warm, safe place to rest and food to nourish your bodies."

Roan bowed deeply to the woman. "We thank you from the bottom of our weary hearts. Such goodness should be repaid with honesty. I am Roan, son of Ryan, soldier of the palace guard. I was escorting my lady here when we were set upon by thieves who took our horses and provisions. We barely escaped with our lives. We are also being pursued by mercenaries eager to capture us and hold my lady for ransom."

The old woman approached them and put her hand under Caritas's chin, tilting her face to the light. "And you, small one, are the cause of all this turmoil?"

Caritas felt tears of weariness and shame spring to her eyes. "I am trying to reach my parents. They are in danger."

"One so small should not shoulder so great a burden alone," the woman said sympathetically.

"It is mine to bear," Caritas replied. When she saw the kindness in the old woman's blue eyes, she decided she could trust these kind people. "I am Princess Caritas, firstborn of the king and queen. I am pursued by Mort, a mercenary in league with my scheming uncle, who would use me as a pawn against my parents. I must take this knowledge to them before it is too late."

The old woman held Caritas's gaze a moment longer. "Gwen, release the other dogs. Our princess must rest safely."

She turned to Roan and added, "And you, young man, seem very young to have been entrusted with so great a mission."

Roan bowed again before responding, "My life belongs to my princess."

"I was not questioning your loyalty, son. It is just that you carry a greater burden than the princess."

"I also strive to make my father proud. Filial piety is a great impetus."

The old woman laughed gently and placed a wrinkled but firm hand on Roan's shoulder. "I see now why they entrusted Her Highness to you. You are brave and clever. I have no doubt you will succeed."

Roan gave Caritas a look that clearly said, "I told you so."

The woman spread her arms in welcome. "Now that I know who my guests are, I welcome you again to Woodhaven. Make yourselves at home. Our house shall serve you its best. I am known to all as Grandmother Linden and this is Grandfather Linden. You have already met our Gwen."

Caritas and Roan both expressed their genuine gratitude.

Caritas and Roan were served fresh eggs, bread, and

fruit. Grandfather Linden brought in fresh warm milk. They ate and drank eagerly while Gwen peppered them with questions. Caritas felt drawn to the peasant girl. Her strength and confidence and . . . joy were evident and enviable.

After their breakfast, Gwen made up a bed for Caritas near the fireplace, while Roan retired to a small guest house. Gwen chatted with Caritas, who felt warm and safe for the first time in many nights.

Chapter 14

C arrie was interrupted by a call to dinner from her mother.

As had been her habit lately, Carrie picked at her food. She didn't feel hungry. Her mother felt her forehead to make sure she wasn't feverish. After dinner had been cleaned up and Sammy had been tucked in for the night, Carrie curled up in the living room with a book. Mrs. Adams sat next to her.

"Sweetie," she addressed Carrie, "won't you tell me what's bothering you?"

Carrie put the book down and shrugged.

"I know you were upset after checking your email. Is that part of what's wrong?" she asked.

"Yeah," Carrie said noncommittally. "I guess so."

"Is there anything I can do to help?" her mother asked.

Carrie shook her head. Mrs. Adams put her arm around her oldest and held her tightly. "I know it's hard, sweetie. I'm sorry about that."

Carrie sat uneasily, not really knowing how to respond.

"What do you miss most?" Mrs. Adams asked.

"Just my friends, I guess," Carrie said, even though in her heart she knew it wasn't true. "You just can't replace people, you know?"

Her mother sighed and leaned Carrie's head against her shoulder.

"I know, Carrie. I know."

And for the first time it occurred to Carrie that her mother really did know.

❧

Two more weeks flew by. Even though the semester was progressing in earnest, there were still plenty of non-homework-related things to do.

Jonny had started playing football with a team of local homeschoolers. Dad loved his new job. He vastly preferred the private Catholic college, with its pretty campus on the river, to the college position he had left in Washington. Mom had settled into the house and was now preparing for the new baby, due to arrive in a few more weeks.

This was now "home," Carrie noted with some bitterness. But in her mind "home" was still the place she had left behind. And even if she never said it to anyone, "home" was where Cecilia was. *And that would never be here,* she thought.

Carrie was aware that her parents talked about her in low voices and glanced anxiously in her direction. She didn't pay much attention. She was getting her school work done. Her grades were okay. She did her chores and helped with Sammy. In her mind, she was doing what needed to be done. But that was all.

At the next homeschool gathering, Carrie sat at a table, gazing off into space. The usual volleyball game had begun, indoors this time. She saw Jenny, but she didn't go over to talk to her. Being alone was easier. People required effort. She quietly slipped back into her story.

Caritas opened her eyes to the late afternoon sunlight. She swung her legs around until her feet touched the cold flagstones as she hauled herself up from her straw mattress. Her borrowed nightdress was soft and warm. She stepped gingerly to the door and looked outside. The garden was at peace, everything ordered. The only thing that seemed out of place was a large pile of fur between the raised beds. As she watched, a vague shape in the pile shifted and a dog raised its head and looked at her. The animal looked less terrifying than it had earlier. Seeing its face in a calmer light, Caritas realized that the dog looked almost friendly, like the palace hounds she had rolled around in the grass with when she was younger.

A movement and a scent caught her attention at the same time, distracting her. The aroma was that of a hearty stew and home-baked bread. The movement was that of two people making their way toward the house. Roan and Gwen passed the dogs, who wagged their tails at their mistress.

Roan looked tousled and droopy-eyed. He had straw stuck in his hair and Caritas giggled at the sight of him. She grabbed a pile of clothes next to the bed and went to get herself ready.

The two entered and Caritas, wearing clothes borrowed from Gwen, greeted them with a smile. As they sat down at the table, a door swung open and Grandmother and Grandfather Linden entered with a steaming pot and loaves of bread. Gwen jumped up to help. She passed around deep wooden plates, which Grandmother loaded with stew, while Grandfather cut thick slices of bread and offered them fresh vegetables and fruit. Caritas's mouth watered. They all paused to give thanks for the meal and then ate heartily.

After they had finished the simple but delicious meal, Caritas and Roan were ready to discuss the serious business of their journey. Gwen thought they should wait a few more days to give their trail time to grow cold. Grandmother thought it would be wise to smuggled them to another cabin, closer to the palace, where they might be safer. Grandfather suggested that Caritas and Roan should at least wait until some word on the location of the royal party arrived. Caritas recognized they meant well with their advice, but she was adamant: they must continue as soon as possible. There was no time to waste.

She made this clear to her hosts, who reluctantly agreed. In the morning, Gwen and Grandfather would take them on the road as far as the outskirts of the castle. They would have to hide in a wagon, among the vegetables barrels, sacks, and tools destined for the market.

After everyone helped clear the table, Gwen went to check on the animals. Roan talked with Grandmother and Grandfather about a few mutual acquaintances, eager to hear any news.

Caritas sat in front of the fire, alone with her thoughts.

Chapter 15

❦

Carrie was startled when Jenny bounded up and sat down next to her. "We're going to start another game soon. Want to play?" she asked.

"Um, I, uh . . ." Carrie couldn't figure out how to finish that sentence.

"Please?" Jenny pleaded, grabbing Carrie's hand. "We need another girl on our team."

Since Carrie couldn't think of an excuse fast enough, she looked at Jenny and said, "Okay."

"Yay!" Jenny exclaimed. She helped a reluctant Carrie up and practically dragged her to the volleyball court.

"Hey, everyone," Jenny yelled to the kids milling around, "this is Carrie. She just moved here. And she's on *my* team."

It seemed to Carrie that everyone was staring at her, but with Jenny hanging on to her elbow, she felt less nervous than she would usually be.

The faces were kind or curious. There was no hostility or awkwardness. Two boys approached her. They were both really good-looking, Carrie noticed, blushing.

"Hey, Carrie," said the taller one, "welcome to Green Bay."

He held out a hand, which she shyly shook.

"I'm Tommy and this is my brother, Nick. You're on our team." He smiled brightly, showing her a line of white, even teeth.

"Um, thanks," she said quietly, still feeling shy.

"Well, we're going to round up more teammates," said Tommy, as he and Nick ran off. When Carrie glanced at the net, she noticed Ben watching her. He gave her a half-smile and nodded. She smiled back.

A few minutes later, the game started. There were no real stars, Carrie noticed, and no real pressure. Everyone seemed happy to be there, enjoying the good-natured ribbing between teams and the many high-fives among teammates. On Carrie's team, the only really good players were Nick and Tommy. She idly wondered if Brent played volleyball or if he played any sports at all. He never had emailed her. Carrie strained her memory to try to remember what he looked like. Her brain didn't have a clear picture anymore—and she had last seen him only a couple months ago.

Suddenly, for the first time in the game, she saw the ball hurtling toward her. She clasped her hands together and nervously whacked it. It popped up and flew toward Nick, who hit it over the net.

The other team couldn't get to it in time, giving a point to Carrie's team.

"Woo-hoo," Nick shouted. "Game point!" He approached, hand in the air. "Good assist," he complimented her. Carrie high-fived him shyly.

Jenny claimed her company after the game. "Good game!" she told Carrie. Carrie smiled, unsure what to say.

"It's almost time to go, but can I have your email address?" Jenny asked. "I need some book recommendations for a class and I know you read a lot."

"Sure," said Carrie uncertainly.

On the drive home, Carrie sat in the front seat, next to her mother.

"I saw you playing with the other teens," her mother remarked, smiling. "I'm proud of you."

"Thanks," Carrie muttered. She wasn't sure how she felt about it. She felt almost guilty, as if her joy in her new friends was a betrayal of her old friends. She shook her head with irritation. *It's complicated,* she told herself . . .

Caritas and Roan were settled snugly among barrels and sacks, hidden from anyone looking at the cart. There would be trouble, however, if someone started moving things around.

Caritas found herself listening tensely to any sounds on the road.

Roan nudged her arm gently and she glanced at him.

"Don't forget to breathe," he whispered with a smile, trying to ease the strain.

Caritas closed her eyes and let out her breath. She smiled back at him and nodded. He was wearing clothes borrowed from Gwen's grandfather. Caritas had only seen him in his soldier's uniform. He looked somewhat uncomfortable in civilian clothes, but Caritas noticed his posture and bearing, even among the barrels and sacks, were still that of a soldier.

Caritas had borrowed clothing from Gwen. The peasant's clothes were lighter than the rich fabrics she had been wearing, and Caritas was grateful in the warm, tightly packed cart. Caritas felt freer in Gwen's clothes, as if somehow they came with a lighter burden than her own gown and cloak.

Caritas heard a voice hailing and felt the cart rumble to a halt. Gwen's grandfather responded cheerily; then two other male voices answered. Her heart froze.

The car slowed to a stop in the driveway. Carrie looked out the window and sighed. They were back at the house. Carrie still couldn't bring herself to call it home.

The next day, she was drying dishes with her mother in the kitchen.

"So, Jenny seems like a nice girl," her mother volunteered.

"Yeah," Carrie agreed.

"Do you guys have much in common?" she asked.

"Some, I guess," she answered indifferently.

Mother pursed her lips. "Is it still hard to be here?" she asked.

Carrie looked her mother in the eyes and answered firmly, "Yes."

Her mother sighed. "Would you really be happier if we moved back to Washington?"

"Maybe. Probably," she replied. She felt surprisingly guilty for her answer.

Ben and Jenny had gone out of their way for her, not to mention her parents. They had tried to make her feel welcome, to help her to make friends, to help her settle in. She felt so ungrateful. But at the same time . . .

Some loyalties run deeper, she thought. *That's all.*

Chapter 16

Until her heart found rest, her mind would be restless. And since her mind was restless, she let it wander.

After a brief exchange between Grandfather and the two other men, the cart rumbled on. Caritas sighed with relief. Some time later the cart stopped again. Then the sacks were lifted and Caritas and Roan stepped out.

"The road was crawling with soldiers," Gwen informed them. "They said they were palace guard, but their uniforms weren't right. The man in charge was tall and dark, and he barked when he spoke."

"Mort," Roan and Caritas replied together.

Caritas clenched her teeth so hard her jaw ached. The greed that made him so persistent in his chase angered her.

Gwen's grandfather continued, "It looks like there's an encampment of mercenaries outside the town, maybe inside too."

Caritas's brow furrowed as she remarked, half to herself, "That can't be right."

"The palace guard rarely ventures outside the palace," Roan informed her. "It would be the watch's job to protect the town itself."

"And we don't know that the mercenaries are in the town. They could be just outside," Gwen cut in.

"Your Highness, it's not too late to turn back . . ." Roan began. He stopped when he saw Caritas fold her arms and set her jaw stubbornly. No words were needed—he could read the mulish determination in her stance.

Roan sighed, "Very well, Your Highness. We'll need to exercise the utmost caution."

Caritas nodded, "If we wait we could sneak through under cover of night."

"Or," Gwen interjected, "we could march right through in daylight. After all, they'll be looking for a princess and her bodyguard, right? Not for two sisters and their brother joining their family in town."

"What's your idea?" asked Caritas.

"We have family in town. I live with my grandparents to help them with the chores, but my parents and brothers and sisters live within sight of the palace itself. I'm well known by the watch and the guards, as I come and go so frequently. If I tell them you're my brother and sister, or my cousins, they'd have no reason not to believe me. I have many brothers and sisters," she added.

Roan nodded with approval, "A fair plan."

"Yes, but if someone were to discover us, we'd be captured immediately," Caritas added cautiously.

"However, this way we just need to get to the town gate. One of my brothers is on the gate guard. They answer directly to the palace guard themselves. Or he could put us in touch with the watch, if you would prefer that," Gwen offered.

Caritas stood still, eyes closed, trying to work out in her own mind what course of action would be best.

"My lady," Roan addressed her, "what we're about to do is already dangerous enough. Having others on our side can only be helpful."

Caritas found herself agreeing reluctantly.

"Thank you, Gwen," Caritas said solemnly. "When I find my family, you will be rewarded for the risks you are taking for me."

Gwen gave her a half-smile. "Don't thank me yet. We still need to get to the gate for this plan to work. And I'm not doing this for a reward. I'm doing it for a friend."

Caritas smiled at Gwen's meaningful look. "Lead on, my friend," she told Gwen.

After saying farewell to Grandfather and watching the farm cart rattle off, the three made their way on foot through the woods. Gwen carried a basket of apples and another of flowers. Caritas didn't understand the sense of carrying extra weight, but as she started to ask, Gwen put her finger to her lips.

The rattling dishes brought Carrie back.

Time seemed to slow down. School work, chores, dealing with her brothers, waiting in vain for an email from Meg .... She did receive an email from Jenny asking about her favorite books. Carrie hadn't answered yet.

On Thursday it was raining hard, so they all stayed indoors.

Mom put Sammy down for a nap. Jonny was at the computer, researching his history paper. Carrie was at the dining room table agonizing over her math lesson. From the corner of her eye she saw both of her parents walking in. They sat next to her.

Carrie put her book aside, seeing in their faces that they were about to say something serious. Dad's normally cheerful demeanor was somber and Mom's eyes were red.

Mom looked at Dad and nodded slightly.

"Carrie," her father began.

Carrie sat up straighter.

"Your mother and I know that you're having trouble settling in here. It's very hard for us to see you hurting like this. I'm not sure what else we could do to make you more comfortable here. You have your own room. We've tried to help you make friends . . . ."

He paused, as if waiting for a response. Carrie simply didn't have one.

Mom leaned over and took Carrie's hand. "Sweetie, we talked to your Aunt Joan in Port Orchard. She said she'd be willing to let you live with her if you want. We know it isn't Bremerton, but it's close, and you would see your old friends as often as you wanted. Would that be better?"

Carrie felt dizzy. She'd pictured it all before: going back, being with her old friends. But it had never been an actual possibility. She'd see Meg again and Brent and . . . *Cecilia*. A corner of her mind whispered. *Cecilia*.

Her mother and father looked at her, waiting for a response.

"Can . . . can I sleep on it?" she stammered.

"Of course, sweetie. We don't have to rush into anything," her mother reassured her as she squeezed her hand.

After they left the room, Carrie sat, stunned. *Green Bay . . . or Bremerton? Meg . . . or Jenny? Her family . . . or Cecilia?* How could she choose?

Chapter 17

The next day at the homeschool gathering, Carrie sat in a corner as her mother chatted with the Mrs. Jackson. Her mother looked particularly tired. Jenny was there, too, but Carrie didn't go over. Her choice weighed too heavily on her mind.

Caritas, Roan, and Gwen stood behind the tree line, gazing into the enemy camp. They could see Mort striding through the camp, barking orders at his men.

They observed the camp for a few moments before Caritas asked cautiously, "Can we go around?"

Roan thought for a moment and answered, "Mort knows what he's doing. He'll have the town gate covered, no matter which direction we approach from."

"What about the road? Surely he wouldn't dare accost us in a public place with so many witnesses present," Caritas offered.

"It would make no difference to a man like him," Roan

responded with disdain. "He doesn't care about that sort of thing. He knows folks shy away from men in uniform. And if they look like they know what they're doing, people would assume they are executing legitimate business."

Caritas shuddered slightly at the word "executing."

"We need one of their uniforms," interjected Gwen suddenly.

Both Roan and Caritas looked at her in surprise.

"One uniform won't cover three of us," Roan pointed out sarcastically.

"It doesn't need to," she replied.

She pointed at the camp. There were some people in civilian clothes.

"I've been watching. The civilians are selling merchandise, which I expected. It appears that the sellers have a uniformed escort. So, our disguises are here," she picked up the baskets of fruit and flowers for emphasis, "and your uniform is . . . there!" She pointed out a solitary soldier behind one of the tents, smoking a pipe. He was either off-duty or a terribly negligent guard.

After a brief whispered consultation, the three took their places.

Moments later, the idle soldier was approached by the two girls. They appeared to be distressed.

"Oh, good sir, can you help us? A wheel has fallen off our cart and we must get our goods into town in time to sell at the market!"

The guard, upon seeing the two young women, sat up

admiringly. Hearing their plight, he stood up, knocked out his pipe on the heel of his boot, and followed them into the woods.

"And how do you girls intend to reward your rescuer?" he asked with a leer.

"Like this!" Roan said from behind as he whacked the guard on the head with a heavy tree branch. The guard dropped unconscious to the ground.

They relieved the man of his uniform and weapon and tied his hands and feet with one of Gwen's scarves.

Roan dressed himself in the drab gray uniform. He pulled the sword from his belt and tossed it slightly in the air to test its balance.

"What do you think?" Caritas asked mischievously.

"Not the best I've handled, but it'll do. I'm just glad to be armed again. Who knows what we'll encounter next?"

"Hi, Carrie," said a voice next to her, pulling her from her reverie. It was Jenny.

"Do you want to take a walk?" she asked.

Caught off guard, Carrie stuttered, "I . . . um . . . I . . . uh . . ."

"Come on," Jenny said, grabbing her arm and pulling her up. "We can go watch the soccer game."

"Okay, then," Carrie agreed, surprised.

It was a beautiful, sunny October day. The air was crisp but not too cold.

"See?" said Jenny. "It's a beautiful day out here."

"Mm-hmm," Carrie mumbled, her mind elsewhere.

"So, what have you been reading lately?" asked Jenny.

"Um, not too much," Carrie replied. She didn't want to talk. She wanted to think. No, she wanted to go back to where Caritas and Roan were . . . .

"Is something wrong?" Jenny asked, sensing her friend's tension.

"No, nothing," Carrie started to say. Then she met Jenny's eyes, full of concern. "Well . . . there's something I need to figure out and I don't know what to do."

Jenny nodded sympathetically. She put her hand on Carrie's shoulder. "I know you'll do the right thing."

Carrie, grateful for the affirmation, hesitated and then said, "I don't know what the right thing to do is."

Jenny looked at her friend and cocked her head. "Did you ever read *The Ballad of the White Horse?*"

"Sure, I've read it," Carrie replied. "It's really beautiful poetry."

"Okay, so my favorite part is how Alfred, even when he doesn't know if he'll win the battle or not, keeps on fighting. In his mind, he's not allowed to give up. Whenever something bothers me, I just try to remember that no matter what, I have to keep going. Even when it's hard and I don't know what to do. We need to keep fighting for what we love."

Carrie looked at her friend with wide eyes. "Thanks," she said. "I think I know what you mean."

"Yeah," Jenny said. "Not giving up in the face of defeat . . . pretty cool stuff, isn't it?"

"Cool," Carrie echoed. "And . . . and brave."

As they returned to the parking lot, Jenny turned to Carrie.

"You know . . . if there's ever anything you need to talk about, you can always call me, okay?" Jenny said kindly.

Carrie nodded and said, "I will, thanks."

Carrie felt a little guilty. She knew Jenny was trying to be friends with her, maybe trying harder than Carrie deserved. And part of Carrie wanted to reach out to the hand offering help. But part of her was still closed. As she mentally gazed down the road that would lead her, she shivered. It was a cold and lonely path, but Carrie didn't know how to stray from it yet.

❦

Carrie had packed up their lunch things and

was just getting ready to take them to the car when she heard Sammy wailing. Glancing over, she saw him, stomach down on the ground, kicking his legs and screaming at the top of his healthy lungs. She hurried over to her mother, who was surveying the tantrum and breathing heavily as she comforted her son in a low voice.

"What's wrong?" Carrie asked.

"He doesn't want to get into the car," answered her mother with a strained voice. Carrie glanced at her in concern. Her mother tried to smile reassuringly, but she had one hand over her stomach and a sheen of sweat covered her pale face.

Carrie's heart jumped into her throat.

"Are you okay?" Her voice jumped an octave with fear. Her mother wasn't due for two more weeks.

Mom nodded and squeezed Carrie's hand. "I'm just tired. He's so big now. I don't really have the energy to fight with him."

Carrie's eyes narrowed as she watched Sammy's tantrum. "I'll get it. Don't worry. Just sit down for a while," she offered.

"Are you sure?" her mother asked.

Carrie could hear the relief and gratitude in the question.

Carrie nodded and scooped up the still-wailing toddler, who fought with her half-heartedly.

She put her mouth close to his ear and started to whisper. Sammy stopped and listened, resting his head on her shoulder and panting. Then he pouted, but nodded his tear-stained face and allowed himself to be carried back to the van. He whimpered as Carrie gently fastened the straps of his car seat, but he sat patiently for it. Carrie dug into her backpack and produced a chocolate granola bar from her secret stash. Sammy's face lit up as he accepted the treat and he began to nibble contentedly.

Jonny arrived, carrying their lunch bags. Mom squeezed herself into the driver's seat and from the rearview mirror saw Sammy munching quietly.

She turned to Carrie and mouthed, "Thank you."

Carrie smiled in reply.

Jonny climbed in as Mom started the car.

"Where'd he get that?" he asked, eyeing Sammy's treat wistfully.

Carrie started to tell him he ought to mind his own business, but she checked herself and tossed him a granola bar.

"Aw, thanks!" Jonny grinned.

Carrie involuntarily smiled back.

"That's the first time you've smiled in a while," Jonny commented, his own grin widening a fraction, as if he had been personally responsible for his sister's happiness.

Carrie nodded thoughtfully. Maybe, just maybe, they could make this work together. She unconsciously touched her locket. As her fingers brushed its smooth surface, she looked at the place where Cecilia's seat should have been—and the moment was gone. Her indecisiveness returned. She still didn't know what to do. On the way home, Carrie's mind returned to her story.

Chapter 18

W*ith Roan dressed and armed, they made their way back to the camp.*

Roan, Caritas, and Gwen entered at roughly the same point at which they had lured the guard away. Each girl held a basket, and Roan followed at a short distance, keeping his head down.

Gwen slipped right into role, attracting attention, calling out her wares, smiling at everyone. Caritas was sweating from the stress, but Gwen made the sneaking-through-a-heavily-armed-enemy-camp game look effortless, even graceful.

When the other side of the camp and the town gate were in sight, Caritas started to breathe more easily.

"Hey, you there! Stop!"

Caritas's heart leaped into her throat as she heard Mort's gravelly voice commanding them to stop.

She froze. Gwen turned around quickly, almost in a pirouette.

"Can I help you, captain?" she asked, her manner sparkling with charm.

Mort approached them. Caritas could see thunder in

his face. She bent down over her fruit basket, trying to cover her face. What if he recognized her? What if they had put Gwen in horrible danger?

Saturday came and went and Carrie still hadn't made a decision.

On Sunday there was a hint of frost in the air. While her friends and family chatted outside after Mass, Carrie stayed inside. She'd said all her routine prayers and now she just sat there. She was afraid to pray in her own words. What if she still didn't get an answer?

She took a deep breath and began her one-sided conversation. In her own mind, she poured out all her fear and hurt and loss. Tears streamed down her cheeks as she sat in the darkened church, setting everything at the foot of the Almighty. She let herself cry without fear or guilt or shame. And, for the first time, she allowed herself to remember . . . .

❧

It had started out as a common flu, or so they thought. Carrie and Jonny had gotten sick the week before, experiencing all the usual symptoms: fever, headache, nausea, vomiting. It had taken Carrie two days to get over it and one more to recover enough to go back to her school work.

Then Sammy and Cecilia got sick. Sammy bounced back after a day, but after three days, Cecilia started complaining of a stiff neck and whimpering that the lights were hurting her eyes. Her mother called the doctor, who told her to take Cecilia to an emergency room. Mom was calm when she told Carrie to watch her brothers until her father came home. But Carrie could tell from the look in her mother's eyes that something was very wrong.

A few hours later Mr. Adams came home and told them they were going to visit Cecilia at the hospital. Carrie grabbed her coat and helped Sammy get ready. She felt restless and nervous, but she didn't know exactly why. Her father and brothers were unusually quiet as well. It was rare for someone in the family to be so sick and even rarer to go to the hospital. Everyone seemed to need the silence.

When they got to the hospital and met their mother in Cecilia's room, her father hugged her mother closely. Carrie saw her sister hooked up to machines with tubes and a needle in her arm. Her normally sunny, bouncy sister looked pale and exhausted, but she tried to smile when she saw Carrie. Carrie smiled back. She sat by Cecilia's bedside and put her hand in her sister's.

"How are you feeling, sweetie?" she asked.

"Okay," Cecilia whispered.

But she wasn't okay. A doctor came into the room and spoke to Carrie's parents. Carrie heard the phrases "spinal tap," "bacterial meningitis," and "gravely ill," but the words had no meaning for her.

Carrie saw her mother quietly wipe her eyes, and she felt her heart tighten. After the doctor left, her mother and father talked in low voices.

"Carrie, what's wrong?" Cecilia asked in a faint voice.

"Nothing, sweetie," Carrie lied. "Everything's going to be okay."

That night, Mom stayed at the hospital and Dad took the children home. Carrie tried to talk to him about what was wrong, but he was too troubled and distracted. He sent them all to bed early, but Carrie was restless and couldn't sleep or read.

The next day, they went to visit Cecilia again. Mom's eyes were red and swollen, though she smiled at her children. Her father sat with Cecilia as Mrs. Adams took Carrie, Jonny, and Sammy down the hall into a waiting room.

"Your sister is very, very sick," she had told them. Carrie noticed the enormous effort her mother made to keep her voice even. "She needs a miracle to stay with us. So, I need you to pray really hard, okay?"

All three children nodded solemnly.

"And you need to understand that it may be your sister's time . . ." Mom paused and took a deep breath, ". . . your sister's time to go be with Jesus. So, we're each going to take a turn sitting with her, okay?"

Carrie's mouth went so dry she could barely speak. She couldn't process what her mother was telling them.

"No," she had whispered. "No, that can't happen."

Her mother hugged her, tightly and silently.

Sammy went in first with Dad. He was calm, but he couldn't really understand what was happening. He sat next to his sister and fidgeted. Carrie couldn't hear what he was saying.

Jonny's turn was next. Carrie could see the same shell-shocked expression on his face that she felt on her own. He was in there for a while, talking, holding his sister's hand.

And then it was Carrie's turn. She had gone in by herself and sat on the edge of the bed. Cecilia was dozing and Carrie didn't want to wake her. She brushed a few strands of hair off her sister's forehead. Cecilia's eyes fluttered open.

"Hi, sweetie," Carrie whispered.

"Hi," Cecilia whispered back.

"How are you?" she asked.

"I'm going to be okay," she answered weakly.

Carrie fought the urge to cry. She didn't want to frighten Cecilia.

"Carrie?"

"Yes, sweetie?"

"Tell me a story," Cecilia asked.

"Once upon a time," Carrie began, "there lived a royal family in a beautiful castle. There was a king and a queen and their four children: Princess Celia, Princess Caritas, and their two brothers, Prince Jonathan and Prince Samuel. They were very happy together, but their kingdom was in danger. Someone was plotting to steal the throne from the king and queen . . . ."

Carrie continued telling her story for several minutes. Cecilia lay contentedly listening, her little hand moving in Carrie's every once in a while, letting her know her audience was still listening. A wild hope sprang up in Carrie's mind. If she could just keep telling the story, Cecilia would stay here to listen to it. So even after her parents and her brothers returned to the room, she continued the story, whispering so that only Cecilia could hear her. Every chance she got, she told Cecilia another part of the story.

That evening, she begged to stay with her mother and sister instead of going home. *If I can just continue the story,* she thought resolutely, *Cecilia will be okay and maybe even get better.*

But by the next morning, Cecilia had gone to Jesus. Cecilia had died.

❧

When Carrie could cry no more, she sat struggling with all the feelings her remembering had awakened. Deep inside her, she knew she had to let go. Of all the anger, pain, and confusion. Of all the fear and guilt that she should have done more . . . she had to let go. She had to empty her heart of the burden. She pictured herself holding all her feelings, putting them down in front of the altar, and taking a step back.

She sobbed as she raised her eyes to look at the crucifix. She was hoping for a sign, anything to let her know she wasn't alone.

And as she sat there a peace filled the space she'd made in her heart. Everything she'd been struggling with seemed to fall into place. The truths she wouldn't let herself see became clear. She knew what she had to do.

She had been hoping for a roll of thunder or a ball of fire or the voice from heaven. Instead, there was sudden quiet, and it was louder than any sound.

Her father's voice broke the quiet.

"Carrie? Carrie!" he cried with urgency.

Chapter 19

Carrie rushed outside the church to see her mother doubled over, clutching her stomach. Her father was starting the car.

"Mom!" Carrie exclaimed, springing to her mother's side.

Her mother was breathing rapidly. "It's okay, sweetie," she gasped. "It's okay. It's time. Find the boys."

Carrie nodded and whirled around, shaking. "Jonny!" she called. "Sammy!" She sprinted around the church to the playground, calling their names.

She found them and told them quickly, "Mom is . . . she's having . . . she says it's time for the baby."

The boys took off for the front of the church, where Dad was helping Mom into the van.

"Are you okay?" Jonny asked in a trembling voice.

Mom nodded. "My water just broke, so your father and I are going to the hospital."

"Carrie, Mrs. Jackson is going to take you and the boys home." Dad said, "She'll stay with you, but I need you to help her with the boys. Can you do that?"

Carrie nodded despite her shaking. She could do this. "Will you call when . . . ? When anything happens?" she asked.

"Of course," he said. He got into the driver's seat.

Mom rolled down the window. "Be good," she said to them. "I love you!"

"I love you, too, Mom," Carrie said, her vision blurred, her chest heavy with fear. The last time someone had been rushed to the hospital . . . she had never come home.

Carrie shook her head. It wouldn't be the same this time. It couldn't be. *But it might,* a tiny corner of her mind whispered. *It might.*

Carrie felt something in her hand and looked down. Sammy was clutching her hand and looking up at her with wide, frightened eyes.

"Is she going to be okay, Carrie?" he whispered.

Carrie bent down to pick him up. "She's going to be fine. I promise. And when she comes home, there's going to be a baby," she reassured him.

Sammy snuggled his head on her shoulder and nodded as Carrie took him to the Jackson's van.

"So what do we do now?" Jonny asked Carrie when they got home.

Mrs. Jackson was on the phone with her husband.

Jonny flopped down on the couch. Carrie shrugged.

Jonny's face lit up. "Can we watch a movie?" he asked.

Carrie smiled a little. "Knock yourselves out."

Sammy's head popped up to look Carrie in the eye. "Movie?" he asked hopefully.

"Yep," she said.

He wiggled out of her arms and followed Jonny to the basement. Jonny and Sammy started arguing about what movie to watch. Carrie wandered back upstairs. Jenny, who had come with her mother, followed slowly.

Carrie didn't want to watch a movie. She really, really wanted to retreat, to close her eyes and be somewhere else, somewhere where her stomach wasn't in a knot. But she knew she couldn't. Her brothers needed her. She rested her forehead against a door frame, trying to take deep breaths. *What would Caritas do in a situation like this?* she asked herself. *Because I really don't think I can do this as Carrie . . . .*

Lunch, she thought. *The boys will need lunch.* She headed toward the kitchen and noticed Jenny behind her.

"Want to help me make some sandwiches?" she asked.

Jenny smiled. "Just tell me where the peanut butter is!"

Mrs. Jackson walked into the kitchen. "Thank you girls," she said when she saw the sandwiches and apple slices prepared for lunch.

"I'm not sure what we'll do for dinner, but at least we have lunch out of the way," Carrie said.

"There's no need to worry about that, dear. We'll order pizza and have it delivered," Mrs. Jackson said decidedly.

Carrie was taken aback by her kindness. "Okay, that would be great," she agreed.

Mrs. Jackson smiled warmly and patted Carrie's shoulder. "Don't you worry, dear. Everything is going to be fine."

Carrie's back stiffened for a moment. She'd heard that before. Saying it didn't make it true. Then she relaxed. Mrs. Jackson just wanted to be kind.

"Wanna watch a movie?" Carrie asked Jenny.

"Sure," Jenny said, smiling her wide smile

She and Jenny brought lunch downstairs to the basement

"Here's lunch, guys," she announced when

she found the boys sprawled on bean bags in front of the TV. "What are you watching?"

"*Chicken Little*," Sammy replied proudly. "I won."

Carrie looked at Jonny questioningly. Jonny sighed with mock irritation. "I should never have taught him 'rock, paper, scissors,'" he said.

Carrie smiled and she and Jenny settled onto the couch. Carrie had seen this movie before—many times. It was Sammy's favorite, followed by *Cars*. She willed herself to be distracted by the cartoon, but, in her mind, the time dragged on endlessly. When would they hear some news from the hospital?

Chapter 20

S he tried not to think about it. Mom at the hospital. She couldn't wrap her mind around it, and she didn't want to try.

Mort stomped toward them and stood over them. Caritas dared not look at him.

Caritas risked a glance at Gwen, who seemed the picture of composed innocence.

"Flower for your lady, captain?" she asked, smiling coquettishly.

Mort grunted. Caritas could see he was facing Roan. Had he been recognized?

"Stand up straight, soldier," Mort ordered. "You call that a uniform? Where's your sergeant? You should be whipped for sloppiness."

Roan snapped to attention and began to fiddle with his uniform, while Mort threatened punishment for the state of Roan's posture and attire.

Caritas continued to busy herself with her apple basket, trying hard not to be noticed. To no avail.

"You," Mort demanded.

She glanced up, eyes wide. She straightened, holding her basket protectively in front of her.

"How much?" he asked.

Caritas froze, wondering what he was talking about.

"Copper penny a piece, captain," Gwen interjected merrily.

Caritas realized they were talking about the price of apples and calmed down. She nodded in agreement with Gwen.

Mort mumbled something about the high price of apples these days and fished around in a pouch. He threw a penny in Caritas's basket and selected an apple.

"Don't look so scared," he said to Caritas, "I'm not going to eat you."

"Yes, sir," Caritas managed to chirp. "Have a good day, sir."

Mort grunted, turned, and strode off.

Caritas thought she was hearing thunder, but it was only the beating of her heart.

She heaved a deep sigh of relief and nearly laughed, but Roan put a hand on her shoulder. "We're not out of the woods yet," he murmured.

As they tried to maintain an unhurried pace through the camp, Caritas strained to listen for Mort's return. She heard him stop. Caritas glanced back and saw him watching them, his eyes narrowed.

"Hey," he called to them. Caritas could hear recognition in his voice this time.

"Run," she breathed to her companions. The three sprinted for the gate, which they reached before Mort could accost them again.

Caritas noticed that the gate guard had been tripled since she had last seen them. The captain knew Gwen, however. A few whispered words from her and two soldiers whisked them through the gates and to safety.

Carrie felt a smack on her shoulder and opened her eyes. Jonny had swatted her shoulder. "Mrs. Jackson wants to know what you want on your pizza," he said.

"Um, my usual. Mushrooms and onions," she said.

Over Jonny's shoulder, she could see Jenny giving her a puzzled look. "Did you fall asleep?" she asked Carrie.

Carrie blushed. "No," she said, "that's just how I think."

"Oh," said Jenny.

They went upstairs. Soon, the pizza arrived. Mrs. Jackson was setting out paper plates and a mouth-watering aroma emanated from the pizza boxes on the table.

The meal eased the tension Carrie was feeling. Around her, the boys, Jenny, and Mrs. Jackson discussed the homeschool group and upcoming events. Carrie struggled to pay attention, half of her mind at the hospital with her mother, the other half at that hospital back in Bremerton . . . .

Jenny bumped her elbow. "Hey," she said quietly to Carrie, "are you okay?"

"Um, yeah," Carrie replied clumsily. She struggled for words. "It's just . . . been a long week. And I'm tired. And I have this thing to figure out. And . . ."

The phone rang. The sound made Carrie stiffen. As much as she ached to hear news, any news, she was afraid. Mrs. Jackson stood up to answer the phone, but Jonny had already run to pick it up. It was a game he and Carrie had played in the past. As he answered the phone and looked around expectantly, he saw Carrie hadn't moved from her seat. His face fell a little.

But his eyes widened as he heard the person on the other end of the line. "Hi, Dad," he said.

Suddenly it seemed to Carrie that the world had screeched to a halt.

"Sure, she's here. Hang on," Jonny said as he held the phone up to Mrs. Jackson. "He wants to talk to you."

She took the phone. "Hello? . . . Sure . . . I'll do that. Okay. Here, Carrie. It's your father," she added unnecessarily.

Carrie took the phone. "Hello," she said hesitantly.

"Hi, Carrie!" She could hear the joy in her father's voice. "You're a big sister again. Lily Ann was born about half an hour ago. Mom and baby are doing just fine."

The tense feeling in Carrie's chest let go so fast tears came to her eyes. "Wow!" she said with excitement.

"I want to tell your brothers, so don't let the cat out of the bag, okay?" She could hear the warmth and exuberance in his tone. It suddenly occurred to Carrie just how much he loved being a father.

"Sure, Dad," she said.

"Thanks. So, the plan is Mom is going to stay the night at the hospital with the baby, but I'm coming home in a bit. Mrs. Jackson will stay till then. How are you holding up?" he asked.

"I'm fine. Tell Mom . . . tell Mom I love her. When can we see . . ." she couldn't finish the question without giving away the surprise.

"I'm going to try to bring you guys to the hospital tonight, when your mother settles in, okay?"

"That'd be great. See you then."

"Good girl. Can you give the phone to Jonny?" he asked.

"Sure. Bye, Dad."

She held the phone out to Jonny. "It's for you," she said.

Jonny took the phone. "Hello? Hi, Dad. Really? That's awesome! That's great. Sure, no problem. Okay, awesome. Uh-huh. Sammy, Dad wants to talk to you."

Sammy took his turn.

"Hi, Daddy. When are you coming home?" he asked.

Carrie noticed with a smile that Sammy's face was intense with concentration. He wasn't very good on the phone yet. "Oh! What's her name? When is Momma coming home? Okay. Bye."

He handed the phone to Carrie. "I'm done now," he stated.

"Hey, Dad, it's me again," Carrie said.

"Hey, Carrie. So, just keep your brothers up for a bit and I'll come and get you, okay?" he asked.

"Sure, no problem. Love you, Dad," she said from her heart.

"Love you, too, Carrie. See you soon. Bye."

"Bye."

Mrs. Jackson stood in the background, beaming. When Carrie hung up the phone, she swooped in and gave Carrie a big hug.

"Congratulations, dear. What wonderful news."

Carrie smiled tightly. "Yeah, it's great. Dad is going to come pick us up. Did he tell you?" she asked.

"Yes, dear. We'll just sit tight till he gets here, okay?"

"Sure. I'm going to be upstairs."

"Of course, dear."

Mrs. Jackson bustled about, clearing up the paper plates and juice boxes.

Carrie walked slowly up the stairs to her room. *Thank you, God,* she breathed. She wondered if her mother had finished getting the baby's crib ready. She entered her parents' room and saw the crib, set up but without a sheet on the mattress. She opened the baby's dresser drawer to look for a sheet.

"Hey!" a voice behind her startled her and she spun around.

Chapter 21

It was Jenny.

"Hey," Carrie replied.

"My mom told me the big news. Congrats! Little sisters are fun," she said.

"I know," said Carrie, more sharply than she intended.

"Oh," said Jenny, taken aback. "Did you want another boy?"

Carrie looked at her in surprise. "No, not at all. I mean, I had a sister, so I know that little sisters are fun," she explained.

"Oh," Jenny said as she sat on the bed. "What happened?"

"She died," Carrie said shortly. "Bacterial meningitis."

"I'm sorry," Jenny said softly.

"Yeah. It's okay," Carrie said.

The girls sat in silence for a moment.

"So," said Jenny, "when do you get to see the baby?"

"Dad is coming to pick us up soon."

Carrie, frustrated in her search for a sheet, sighed and flopped down on the bed next to Jenny.

"Are you gonna be all right?" Jenny asked tentatively.

"I think so," Carrie answered with a shrug.

"Well, if you need to talk, let me know, okay?" she asked.

"Okay." Carrie paused. "Thanks, Jenny."

Carrie, Jenny, and the boys had gone to the basement to play cards when they heard the front door open and Dad call out, "I'm home!"

They ran up the stairs, Carrie first.

Carrie's father held out his arms when he saw her, and she ran into a big hug. The boys scrambled into the room behind her and were immediately gathered into what was now a big group hug.

"Go get your coats," he said when he loosened his hold on them. "We're going to go meet your sister."

The boys ran upstairs for their coats and Carrie followed more slowly, listening as her father thanked Mrs. Jackson for her help and Mrs. Jackson called Jenny. Carrie passed Jenny on her way out. Jenny hugged her enthusiastically.

"Congratulations," she said.

"Thanks again," Carrie said, returning the hug.

Carrie grabbed her coat off the hanger in her closet and her backpack off her chair. It was a small backpack with her "emergency supplies": ten dollars, three granola bars, a notebook and pen, and a small hair brush. She paused, then grabbed her copy of *The Hobbit* and squeezed it into the bag.

She joined her brothers at the front door. They bundled into the van and were off to the hospital. For the first time since that afternoon, Carrie looked at the time. It was after eight o'clock.

Carrie was sure her father was speeding, or perhaps it was just her own heart racing. She could not have said why, but she was nervous, and she felt a headache coming on. She closed her eyes.

Once inside the town walls, a guard escorted Caritas, Roan, and Gwen to the palace. There was an air of vigilance inside the town. Everyone on the streets was aware that Mort's forces were outside the gate. The townsfolk were ready at a moment's notice to rise up to protect themselves. Caritas's heart hardened with resolve. These were her people and she would protect them. Why had her parents not ordered them to take safe refuge yet? What were they waiting for?

They reached the palace and one of the palace guards recognized Roan. Gwen quietly took leave of them to find her relatives.

No one had recognized Caritas in her peasant clothes thus far and she was glad of that. She didn't want to draw attention to herself just yet.

When they were inside the palace, Roan left Caritas in a small room near the kitchen. No one was there. She waited anxiously for her friend's return.

Twenty minutes later, he was back, and Caritas could tell from the look on his face that the news wasn't good.

"Your parents aren't here, my lady," he said. "They left two days ago, before Mort's forces arrived."

Caritas slumped down on a bench, tears filling her eyes. All her fear and discomfort and exhaustion . . . for nothing.

"What now, my lady?" Roan asked.

Carrie felt a hand on her shoulder and she opened her eyes.

"Wake up, silly," she heard Jonny say from the seat behind her. "We're here."

Carrie shook off her grogginess and looked around. They were in the hospital parking lot.

They walked in together, blinking in the bright hospital lights.

Dad led them straight to Mom's room, greeting nurses cheerfully on the way. When they entered the room, they saw Mom, looking tired but blissful, holding a little bundle in her arms. She smiled at them.

"Come meet your new sister," she invited them.

Carrie, Jonny, and Sammy crept forward. Mom was looking unusually fragile and pale, despite her smile and assurances. Sammy was the first to arrive at Mom's side, standing on tip-toes and straining to see the new arrival. Mom tilted the baby so that her head was up, facing Sammy.

"Say hello," she prompted gently.

Sammy's brow furrowed and his nose wrinkled as he said, "Hello."

Jonny stood behind him, gazing at the newborn. With a gentle movement, he touched the tiny hand barely visible in the blankets.

"Hi, little one," he whispered.

Carrie stood on the other side of the bed, unable to see the baby's face. She watched her brothers. Her father put a hand on her shoulder and moved her gently to one side. Then he carefully picked the baby up and laid her in Carrie's arms.

"Remember to support her head," he said softly.

Carrie was surprised by how light Lily was. She felt as if she were holding a very fragile doll. Her little face was round and red, and her eyes were closed. Carrie moved her face closer to Lily's, and she could smell the baby's scent, warm and clean. Everything about that peaceful little face was soft and round and perfect.

Suddenly, Lily stirred and her eyes opened. It seemed to Carrie like the baby looked right into her eyes, deliberately and thoughtfully.

"Hello," Carrie whispered. "I'm your sister. I'm going to take care of you."

The tiny infant seemed to consider this, but didn't respond. Carrie gently rocked the infant as a nurse bustled in. The nurse shooed the children away from the bed and pulled the privacy curtain. Suddenly, Carrie felt an awful sense of foreboding sweep over her and she held her sister more tightly.

The nurse emerged a moment later, with a concerned look on her face. She spoke to Mr. Adams in a low voice. The only word Carrie caught was "hemorrhaging." She didn't know what it meant, but Dad apparently did. He nodded gravely and turned to his children as the nurse left the room.

"Carrie, I'm going to need you to take your brothers to the waiting room," he said.

"Why?" Carrie almost choked on the word as her father took the baby from her.

"They need to do something with Mom. I'll explain later," he said. "Trust me, okay?"

"Okay," said Carrie, as calmly as possible with her heart trying to beat its way out of her chest.

"If you go to the nurse's station, a nurse will take you to the waiting room. I have to stay here with Mom and Lily," he instructed.

Carrie nodded and took Sammy by the hand. Jonny followed her, hands in his pockets.

Carrie found the nurse's station and was directed down the hall. The waiting room was, as

Carrie called it, "hospital comfortable." There was a TV with a DVD player, but they hadn't brought any DVDs with them. There were some grown-up magazines, but nothing that interested the children.

They flopped down on the beige couches. Outwardly Carrie looked calm, but inwardly she forced her feelings to freeze, willing herself not to succumb to her irrational terror. *It's going to be okay,* she tried to tell herself. *It's going to be okay.*

But it wasn't, another part of her mind screamed. *It wasn't okay before. Why would it be now?*

Chapter 22

Carrie needed to escape. She closed her eyes.

"No!" Sammy yelled. "No. Stay here. I need you. I don't understand."

Carrie, startled, opened her eyes. Sammy was standing right in front of her, tears streaming down his face. He had her by one arm and he was shaking it with all the strength in his little body.

"What's going on, Carrie?" he wailed. "Is Momma okay? Is Lily okay? Don't go away now. Please!"

Carrie, tears springing into her own eyes, grabbed Sammy and held him close. He needed her to be present. He needed her to be more like Caritas.

"It's going to be okay, Sammy," she tried to comfort him.

He pushed away from her to look into her eyes. "Really?"

"Really," she said with far more conviction than she felt. She reached into her purse. "Here," she said. She pulled out her book and then found the granola bars. She opened one and handed it to Sammy. He sat next to her, snuggling into her side and munching. Jonny was sitting alone on another couch, arms folded sullenly over his chest, staring into space.

Carrie lobbed a granola bar at him and hit him in the chest, startling him.

He smiled at her but she saw the lie in the smile. Even Jonny was worried.

"Here's what we're going to do," said Carrie with an air of authority. "We're going to say a quick prayer for Mom and Lily, and then I'm going to read to you, okay?"

Sammy, eyes wide, nodded solemnly and folded his hands. Sammy was still learning his prayers, but Carrie took her time with the words. They said an Our Father, a Hail Mary, and a Glory Be to the Father. In between prayers, Carrie glanced at Jonny. His head was bowed and hands folded, joining them silently in prayer. When they finished praying, both boys looked calmer.

Carrie picked up her battered paperback and turned to the first page. She began reading the tale of Bilbo Baggins, the hobbit.

Her soothing voice filled the room with a peace she did not feel. Sammy laid his head against her arm. Jonny walked over and sat down next to her as well. They had both read or heard the story about little Mr. Baggins before, so it was a familiar tale that comforted them like a warm blanket. Carrie didn't know how long she read. She didn't mark the passage of time. Her voice rose and fell with the cadence of Tolkien's writing.

And she could see in the faces of her brothers that reading to them was working, allowing them to escape a situation that was too heavy for their young shoulders. They even smiled during the song about breaking Bilbo's plates.

At one point, a nurse in bright pink scrubs poked her head in the room. "Can I get you guys anything?" she asked perkily.

Carrie sat up straight, feeling the burden of speaking for the three of them. "I'd like some water. And we'd like to know what's happening with our mom, please."

The pink nurse nodded and chirped, "Okay. Be right back."

Carrie resumed the story, using different voices for the dwarves and the wizard, but keeping her own voice for Bilbo, and trying not to think of what might happen.

Chapter 23

A different nurse entered the waiting room. She was dressed in flowery scrubs that Carrie thought were pretty. She had a tray with her. She set the tray down on the coffee table and took a seat.

"Hi, guys. I'm Danielle," she said with a gentle smile. "I'm sorry no one's been in here yet. It's been a little crazy at the nurse's station tonight."

Carrie and the boys nodded, wide-eyed.

"Anyway, I brought you cookies and apple slices and milk and water. I know you've been waiting here for a while."

The children nodded again. Carrie felt comforted by this woman's gentle air of competence.

"I also asked for an update on your mom. It turns out that she had a little problem after the birth. She just needed a minor surgery to fix it up. She's fine now. She's out of surgery and she's doing well. Lily is fine, too. Your dad is with her." At this point Danielle focused on Carrie. "Your mom isn't going to be able to feed Lily right away because of the anesthesia. So you may need to help with that, if that's okay with you."

Carrie managed to choke out, "Sure, I can do that. Our mom is okay, though?"

Danielle smiled again and reached out to put her hand on Carrie's shoulder. "Honey, she's going to be just fine. This must have been really scary for you guys. But everything is going to be fine now."

Carrie's throat felt very dry.

"Now," said Danielle, suddenly a little more business-like, "your mom is sleeping and your dad is in the room with her. They did want to see you. So eat up your snack and I'll be back to take you to the room in about ten minutes, okay?"

The three children nodded again.

"Thank you, Danielle," Carrie said.

Danielle smiled cheerfully and left the room.

Jonny attacked the food with an appetite. Sammy sighed and rested his head against Carrie. She could feel his little body relaxing against hers. She, too, felt suddenly exhausted.

She exhaled slowly, "They're okay. Thank God, they're okay."

She looked down at Sammy. "Do you want me to read some more?"

He shook his head and mumbled something that sounded like "Un-uhn."

"Do you want a cookie?" she asked him.

"Mm-hmm," he mumbled.

She leaned and managed to get a cookie off the plate without moving him. She slipped the cookie into his hand. He drowsily brought it up to his mouth, taking little bites, till his eyes closed and his whole warm body relaxed against Carrie's.

"Is he asleep?" asked Jonny with his mouth full of apple slices.

Carrie nodded.

Jonny grabbed the cookie plate and brought it close to Carrie. She took a couple cookies. "Thanks," she told him.

"No problem," he grinned. "Good story by the way," he remarked

"Yeah," she agreed.

"I think I know what you meant before," he said.

"Huh?" asked Carrie with some confusion.

"The whole thing about escaping. When you go off into your own world, you're telling yourself a story, right?" he asked.

"Yeah, I guess," she answered.

"Well, when you were reading to us, I was really scared, but it gave me something else to think about, you know?" Jonny reflected.

Carrie smiled and agreed again, "I know."

"Well, I guess you can do that, but you don't need a book or anything, right?" he asked.

Carrie nodded thoughtfully before answering, "Yep."

"That's cool," Jonny said.

Carrie smiled again. "Thanks," she said, pleased.

"Maybe sometime you could tell me one of your stories," he asked.

"We'll see."

"Okay."

At that moment Danielle arrived. "Are you guys ready?" she asked.

Carrie nodded. But she couldn't move without disturbing Sammy. She carefully shifted Sammy around, gathering him into her arms with his head on her shoulder. She hoisted him up without waking him.

Danielle nodded appreciatively. "Well done," she commented.

Carrie smiled.

Danielle led them down the long hallway. They entered Mom's room again. The light was dim, and Carrie could see her father, looking more tired than she ever remembered seeing him. He was holding the bundle of blankets that swaddled Lily, rocking her absently. Her mother looked pale and worn. Her eyes were closed and her breathing seemed shallow to Carrie.

Danielle put her hand on Carrie's arm. "There's

a cot in the corner, on the other side of the bed. I figured some of you might be tired. You can put your brother down there," she offered.

Carrie carefully laid Sammy down and pulled off his shoes. He barely stirred, except to turn onto his side, the way he liked to sleep. Carrie laid the shoes on the floor next to him and approached her father.

He smiled wanly.

"I can hold the baby for a bit, if you want to rest," she suggested.

"Thank you, Carrie," he whispered. He handed her the little bundle.

Jonny flopped down in one of the room's two chairs and Dad rested next to Sammy on the cot. Danielle was checking the monitors by Mom's bed. As Carrie held Lily, she realized she was the only family member in the room fully conscious at this point. Danielle came over and put a hand on Carrie's arm.

She smiled down at the baby and whispered, "We don't usually allow so many guests in one room, but this is an unusual situation, so we'll make an exception. Your mother was able to feed the baby before surgery, but she'll need to eat again in about half an hour. I'll bring a bottle for you, okay?"

Carrie nodded, feeling very grown-up.

"Will you be all right here by yourself?" she asked.

Carrie looked down at the sleeping newborn and then up at Danielle. "We'll be fine," she told the nurse.

"Very good. Feel free to hit the nurse's call button if you need anything, okay?" she said.

"Got it," Carrie said with more confidence than she felt.

And then Danielle was gone. Carrie slowly walked over to the empty rocking chair with her brand new sister and sat down. As she looked into the red, beautiful little face, she felt the full weight of the responsibility in her arms.

"It's all right, Lily," she whispered, "I'm here. Everything's going to be okay."

Carrie sat bolt upright in her chair. As long as she was needed, she would keep watch.

Chapter 24

S he had just begun to let her mind wander, when the little bundle she was holding stirred. She looked down and was slightly surprised to see two deep, dark eyes looking back at her.

"Well, hello," she whispered to Lily. "I didn't know you were up."

Lily continued to stare up at Carrie. She had a puzzled expression, Carrie thought.

"I'm your sister," Carrie said. The puzzled expression didn't change. "We met earlier, but then I had to go away for a little while." Lily continued to stare. "Um, I'm not sure what else to say. You're so new."

Lily blinked slowly.

"That's what I thought." Carrie paused, looking back into the inscrutable little face. "You're pretty quiet, aren't you?"

No answer.

"Would you like to hear a story?"

Lily blinked again.

"Sure you would. Once upon a time, a princess was fleeing through the woods to warn her parents of impending danger, accompanied only by her faithful bodyguard and a loyal young maiden. They tricked the mercenaries into letting them into the palace. Once there, the princess and her bodyguard looked everywhere for the king and queen, but they were nowhere to be found."

Carrie checked on her audience. Lily seemed interested, as far as she could tell. Carrie continued her tale.

"What now, Your Highness?" Roan asked.

"I don't know. Stop calling me that," she said with a catch in her voice.

Roan sat down next to her. "Well, the way I see it, you have two choices. You can drop this pointless anonymity and announce your presence so that you can rejoin your family and maybe help your people, who are besieged outside these walls. Or you can continue the charade that all this has been about warning your parents."

Caritas looked up quickly, angered by Roan's candor. Then she sighed, "You're right, Roan. You've been right this whole time. I will come to the aid of my people and rejoin my parents. But I have something to do first."

Roan nodded and offered, "I will follow you to that end."

"Thank you, my friend."

Carrie glanced down. Her audience was asleep. She looked at her baby sister for a long time. Her newborn face was small and a little scrunched up. Her eyes looked longer than her mouth, which Carrie found a little odd and amusing.

Carrie took the baby over to the bassinet and laid her down gently. Lily stirred ever so slightly, but did not wake.

As Carrie turned to sit down again, she heard a voice calling her name softly. Startled, she looked over and saw that her mother was awake.

She sat down by her mother. "You should rest some more, Mom. All the kids are sleeping."

Mom reached out a hand and grasped Carrie's. Her face was drawn with concern. "I'm all right. How are you and the boys?" she asked.

"We're fine, mom. We just sat in the waiting room till the nurse came and got us," Carrie explained.

"I'm sorry about that," she said wearily.

"It's okay, Mom. It's not like it was your fault," Carrie assured her.

Her mother smiled wanly. "Thank you for caring for them. I know it's a big burden to place on you," she sympathized.

Carrie shrugged awkwardly. She didn't know what to say.

"You're growing up so fast, sweetie. I'm so proud of you," she said.

Tears sprang to Carrie's eyes. "Thanks," she whispered.

"Try to get some rest now, okay?"

"Okay, Mom. You, too. I love you."

"I love you, too, sweetie."

Her mother's eyes closed and it seemed to Carrie that she was already asleep.

Carrie walked carefully over to the rocking chair. She leaned back in it and looked around the room at her family: Mom, Dad, Jonny, Sammy, Lily. She felt the old, familiar heartache she had carried for so many months. *Cecilia would have loved to be here,* she thought. *She would have loved to see the new baby. She would have comforted Sammy when he was frightened. She would have perched next to me while I rocked Lily to sleep.*

It wasn't fair. Even with the new baby, there was a hole in their family. Lily couldn't fill it. No one could.

Chapter 25

Tears coursed their way down Carrie's cheeks. She jumped when the door opened softly. Danielle came in and smiled apologetically when she saw Carrie's surprised look. She bustled around almost silently, checking monitors. Carrie tried hard not to stare, feeling it was rude.

Danielle beckoned to Carrie. Carrie got up and followed her out the door. Danielle's face went from business-like to concerned when she saw Carrie's tear-streaked face in the bright hallway light.

"Are you okay?" she asked.

Carrie nodded.

"Is there something wrong?" Danielle persisted.

Carrie shrugged again, and then decided she was probably going to cry whether she talked or not. "My little sister died last year and I still miss her. She would have loved this."

More tears escaped, in spite of Carrie's efforts. She swiped at them angrily with her sleeve.

"I'm so sorry. I didn't know that," Danielle said as she wrapped a surprised Carrie up in a strong hug. "I'd love to tell you it's going to be okay, but you'll always hurt a little. It's the price we pay for loving."

Carrie nodded.

Danielle released her and laid a sympathetic hand on the side of Carrie's face. "Let me know if you need anything, all right?"

Carrie nodded again, gulping.

"I do need to talk to you real quick. Is that okay?" asked Danielle.

"Sure, what's up?" Carrie managed in between gulps.

"Lily will need to be fed soon. Who should I wake up for that?" she asked.

"I'll probably be awake. Just let me know when it's time."

"Are you sure?" Danielle asked seriously. "You've been awake a lot already tonight."

"I don't think I'll be sleeping anyway and everyone else looks pretty beat," Carrie observed.

Danielle nodded thoughtfully. "Okay. I'll bring in a bottle. And if any of you need anything, you let me know right away."

"Okay."

Danielle placed a sympathetic hand on Carrie's shoulder. "Try to get some rest, all right?"

"Sure," Carrie acquiesced wearily. She wouldn't, but what else was she supposed to say?

Danielle nodded encouragingly and then went about her business.

Carrie went back into the room. Everyone was soundly asleep. She sat in the rocking chair, silently swinging herself forward and back, forward and back. Her stomach growled. The snack tray that Jonny had brought with them "just in case" still had a few browning apple slices on it.

Carrie brought these back to her chair and gazed at Lily as she munched on the apples.

≈

A hand on Carrie's shoulder woke her with a start. She didn't know when she'd drifted off, but now she was looking up into Danielle's face.

"Are you sure you want to get up?" the kind nurse asked.

Carrie nodded. She would do this. It was her responsibility this time.

Danielle laid Lily in Carrie's arms. Then she handed her the bottle and showed her how best to hold it for the baby. Lily caught on right away. She snuggled into Carrie's arms and worked her tiny lips around the bottle's nipple.

Danielle watched and smiled with approval. She left Carrie to feed the baby while she read the monitors and wrote some notes on the chart.

As Carrie watched the baby eat, she marveled. Lily felt like she weighed hardly anything at all. Yet there she was, focusing on a task she was just learning as Carrie held her. She was only a few hours old and she was already learning. It took Carrie's breath away.

Gradually, Carrie felt Lily relax and her eyes drifted shut. She no longer pulled on the bottle and her breathing became deeper. Danielle came over and looked at her. She smiled, lifting the baby out of Carrie's arms and laying her in the bassinet.

Then she came and sat next to Carrie, saying, "Okay, in about an hour I'm going to make sure that the medication has cleared your mom's system. Then she'll be able to nurse Lily herself every three hours or so. Pretty soon, Lily will have her own schedule and she'll let you know when she's hungry. But for right now, you should try to get some sleep. Later we can talk about when everyone's going home."

"Okay," Carrie agreed.

Danielle patted her on the shoulder and left.

Chapter 26

As Carrie relaxed into the chair, faces floated before her eyes. She saw Gwen and Lily, Roan and Jonny, Dad and Mom and Ryan, Sammy and Cecilia, Ben and Jenny . . . . Her confused mind was abruptly filled with clarity. She had to finish her story. She reached into her bag and pulled out her notebook. Hunched over the notebook in the rocking chair, she started writing. Her adventures with Roan spilled out onto the lined paper, chronicling her own stubbornness and anxiety through Caritas.

Caritas made her way through the palace halls to the door leading to her favorite garden. All the flowers were in full bloom and a warm breeze wafted through, swaying the blossoms and knocking the bumble bees off course. Caritas strode through, plucking the most beautiful blooms. Then, slipping off her necklace, she used the chain of her locket to bind the stalks together. Bouquet in hand, she made her way down the halls to a small, secluded courtyard. A white marble monument of a weeping angel guarded a gravestone.

Caritas laid her flowers down at the grave. "Hello, sister," she whispered. "I miss you. All the time I was forcing my way here, it was really because I wanted to find you. But you're gone. I know you're in a better place than I could ever give you. I love you, little one. Rest in peace. You'll always be in my heart. Good-bye."

Caritas bowed her head for a moment and wept. She wept not for the child, but for herself, for her own loss. She believed her sister was in a place where no one could ever hurt her. Caritas still carried the pain of her loss, but now she was also full of peace.

After a moment she raised her head, ready to rejoin Roan and her people.

Out of the corner of her eye, she caught a shadow moving among the stillness.

Caritas whirled around to find herself face to face with Mort.

"There's nowhere to run now, princess," he remarked with a smirk.

"No matter," Caritas said through clenched teeth, "I'm not running anymore."

Mort charged Caritas, knife in hand.

"Roan," she screamed.

Roan ran into the courtyard as Caritas dodged Mort's initial thrust. Mort grabbed her arm. Caritas threw her elbow into his face, smashing his nose. Drops of his blood stained her dress. He swore and wrestled with her as she struggled to free herself from his grasp. Then Roan was there, with his arms around Mort's neck, throwing him to the ground. Mort and Caritas hit the ground together, and his grip loosened. She rolled away in time to see him kick himself free of Roan's grasp. Caritas, in a flying leap, landed on Mort's back, foiling his attempt to get up and knocking the wind out of him. Roan had recovered and grabbed one of Mort's arms, pinning him to the ground. Caritas grabbed the other arm, bringing the felon's wrists together and successfully immobilizing him.

"Beaten at last," Roan declared.

Caritas untied a scarf Gwen had lent her, and they bound Mort's arms with it.

Roan hauled the mercenary to his feet.

Caritas stood in front of him. Even in the face of captivity Mort sneered at her.

"You can no longer hurt me," she informed him.

"You don't know that. I'll be there, when you're alone, darkening your thoughts and filling you with fear. I'll haunt your dreams. You'll never be safe from me," he threatened.

Caritas shook her head. "No, I'm done with you. I have people who need me and love me. You can't touch us," she asserted confidently.

The sneer left Mort's face as Roan forced him to move. Pale and powerless, Mort had met his match in the young man. As they went through the castle, Roan called for his comrades. Soon Mort was surrounded by a dozen men.

"What now?" one of them asked Roan.

"That would be up to Her Highness," Roan said, with a bow in Caritas's direction.

The soldiers turned a confused gaze toward Caritas, who, still in peasant's clothes, stood tall and smiled graciously at them. Realizing that they were in the presence of royalty, the soldiers bowed, even forcing Mort into a position of homage.

A ranking captain stepped forward. "My lady, forgive us for not recognizing you sooner."

"That is all right, captain," she said, "I haven't been myself lately,"

"What are your orders, my lady?" he asked.

"First, lock this ruffian away in the deepest dungeon. He has attempted to harm me and my brothers on more than one occasion. No doubt his men are camped outside the walls planning harm to my parents as well."

The captain bowed in acquiescence. "And what of the mercenaries outside the wall, my lady?" he inquired.

"Gather the palace guard, the town guard, the watch, and as many soldiers as you can. Drive them into the forest," she commanded.

The soldiers smiled at the news.

"When you have completed that task, then scour the forest for the marauders who nest there. My subjects deserve to live and sleep without fear," she instructed.

"It shall be done, my lady," he said.

"Very good, captain. And when that business is finished, bring me an armed escort. I must rejoin my family," she said.

"Of course, my lady," he responded with another respectful bow.

"Thank you, captain. I will go to my rooms now," she added.

The captain assigned a four-man escort to Mort, who now looked smaller and less threatening. The rest of his men scattered to pass on to others the orders Caritas had given. Within minutes, Roan and Caritas found themselves alone.

"Aren't you going with them?" she asked.

"As your handpicked bodyguard, I cannot in good conscience leave you, my lady. Also, I am not subject to orders from anyone except my father and members of the royal family."

Caritas smiled. "I'm glad of that. But in truth you don't always follow my orders."

"Perhaps we can agree that sometimes that is for the best?" Roan asked.

"Yes, we can agree on that. However, if I order you to get some food and rest after a taxing journey, would you obey?" she inquired.

"Yes, my lady," he said with a smile, "if you give me your word that you will not leave the palace without me by your side."

"I would not have it any other way, my brave young captain," she promised.

"Ah, but I am just a lowly corporal . . ." he interjected quickly.

Caritas silenced him with a gesture. "As the firstborn of the royal family, it is within my power to confer honors on those deserving of them. And you are more than worthy of a more prestigious title, Captain Roan," she stated with pleasure.

Roan glowed with pride at his swift promotion. "Well, I cannot wait to see my father's face when he hears this news."

Caritas laughed, "Neither can I." Then reaching a hand out to him, she added, "Thank you, my friend, for everything."

"It was my pleasure, my lady," he said with genuine warmth.

He took her hand and they gazed into each other's eyes, silently resolved never to be separated from the other again.

And, as Carrie dotted the last period, a sense of accomplishment washed over her. All was right in one of her worlds. Now to make things right in the other.

Chapter 27

Carrie looked up. Dad was sitting next to Mom, holding her hand and talking in a hushed voice. Jonny and Sammy were still asleep. Light was streaming in through the windows. Dad and Mom looked over at Carrie and smiled.

She rubbed her tired eyes and got up. She stopped to look in the bassinet, where Lily was awake and gazing up with the same deep stare Carrie had seen during the night. Carrie walked to her mother's bed and sat beside her.

"How are you feeling?" she asked.

"Better," her mother replied. "They want to keep me here for a little longer, but I can nurse Lily and hold her. They said that everything is okay now."

"That's great," Carrie said with relief.

Her father put an arm around her and hugged her. "I heard you were quite the little caretaker last night."

Carrie smiled and shrugged. "I did my best."

Her father kissed her on the forehead and gave her a bear hug. "It sounds like you did more than that. Thank you."

Her mother grasped her hand. "I'm so proud of you, Carrie."

Carrie blushed. "Thanks," she muttered, "Um, can I ... I mean ... um ..."

"What is it, Carrie?" her mother asked.

"I'm going to need to call Aunt Joan when we get home," she finally said.

Her parents looked at each other anxiously.

"I've thought about going back to Washington, and, I mean, it would be great to be closer to Cecilia and Meg and all, but I would miss Jonny and Sammy and Lily. And I'm making friends here. So I want to stay. But ... can I please ask Aunt Joan to do something for me?" Carrie looked up pleadingly.

"Sure, what is it?" her dad said with relief in his voice.

"Can I ask her to buy a dozen pink roses and put them on Cecilia's grave for me? I can send her the money," she offered.

"Oh, sweetie," her mother enveloped her in a hug. "Of course."

Her father joined the hug just as Jonny and Sammy woke up.

"What's going on?" asked Jonny.

"I'm not going," said Carrie. "I'm going to stay here."

"Not going where?" asked Jonny, still puzzled.

Carrie and her mother looked at each other and laughed.

Her father smiled wide. "Who's hungry for breakfast?" he asked, fully knowing the response.

Both of the boys whirled around and said "Me!" startling Lily. She began to cry. Dad picked her up and handed her to Mom, kissing them both gently on the forehead.

"I'll take the kids down to the cafeteria and get them something to eat. Do you need anything?" he asked.

Mom looked up from comforting the baby, smiling serenely. "No, I'm fine, thanks."

Carrie followed Dad and the boys out the door. They took the elevator to the ground floor and entered the cafeteria, where the smell of eggs and sausage reminded Carrie faintly of her story. Her stomach growled. Carrie felt ravenously hungry from staying up all night.

Everyone grabbed a tray and Dad told them to get whatever they wanted. Carrie opted for eggs, French toast, bacon, and a doughnut, with orange juice. Jonny and Sammy both preferred pastries and cereal. Dad had a huge pile of eggs and bacon and, Carrie noticed with amusement, two cups of coffee on his tray.

After breakfast, they paid another visit to Mom and Lily. Then Dad took them home. He bustled around for a bit, calling the college to tell them he wouldn't be in, washing baby clothes, and packing some of Mom's clothes in a bag. Mrs. Jackson arrived with Jenny, and Dad went back to the hospital.

Carrie went to bed early that night, and woke before anyone else the next morning. *Mom's coming home!* she thought. *And Lily!* She half-consciously reached for her locket before she remembered that she had taken it off when she went to bed. It was the first time she had been without it since the move. She rubbed it thoughtfully as she slipped it over her head.

Chapter 28

Two weeks later, Carrie was in her room rearranging her things. There were still gaps to cover, but they somehow weren't as painful now. Carrie reached up and unclasped the chain holding her locket. She held it in her palm and looked at it. She closed her eyes and remembered Cecilia's last night . . .

A nurse had come into the hospital room and insisted that Mom get something to eat. Mom hadn't wanted to go, but finally did, leaving Carrie alone with Cecilia.

Cecilia lay in the hospital bed, almost translucent, like white marble. Carrie reached into her purse and held something cupped in her hands, smiling mischievously at her sister.

"I have a surprise for you," she said.

"What is it?" Cecilia asked with curiosity.

"I was going to wait for your birthday, but I couldn't wait anymore," Carrie said, holding up a heart-shaped locket. Cecilia gasped softly and reached out her free hand to touch the locket as it dangled from her sister's fingers on a slim chain.

"Carrie, it's beautiful!" she exclaimed.

Carrie was so pleased by her sister's reaction she almost giggled. "Wait, that's not even the best part." Carrie popped open the locket to reveal two tiny pictures, one of herself and one of her sister. "See? Now we'll always be together."

Carrie carefully placed the locket in her sister's hand.

"Carrie," Cecilia said with a sigh, "you'll always be in my heart."

❧

Carrie placed the locket on her nightstand. "Always," she said softly to herself.

Later that evening, Carrie was curled up with a book. She had called Jenny earlier and they were going to get together on Wednesday for a study session. It was the first time Carrie had reached out to her friend and it felt good.

Her father came over, holding Lily, and sat down next to her.

"Can I ask what changed your mind about going back?" he asked gently.

"I just did a lot of thinking. I know that I made a big deal about losing my friends and having to move my stuff and everything, but none of that was really the problem. It was really all about Cecilia. I guess I was still grieving. I still am. But when it all came down to it, what was I going to do? I was just torn. But I figured it out. I have a lot more to lose by leaving you all," Carrie said, stroking Lily's hand with her finger.

"I'm very proud of you," her father said, putting his arm around her shoulders. "Some people live their whole lives without understanding their own motivations."

"Thanks, Dad," she said, laying her head on his shoulder. "That means a lot."

Sammy wandered by in his pajamas, his hair still wet from his bath.

"Momma said you could read me a book before bed," he said to Carrie, climbing into her lap. "Can you read me the one about the little hairy man?"

"You mean *The Hobbit?*" she asked.

"Yes."

"Probably not the whole thing," she chuckled.

He sighed dramatically, "Oh, okay. Just some of it, then?"

"Sure, Sammy."

"Carrie," he said, without moving from his

position on her lap, "please don't go away like Bilbo does, okay?"

"I won't, Sammy. I promise."

"I love you, Carrie."

"I love you, too, buddy. Always."

K. Kelley Heyne

is a homeschooling mom
who was homeschooled
herself. She lives in Wisconsin
with her husband, Peter, and
their four children who keep
her busy and entertained.
In her free time, she writes
articles and novels on subjects
ranging from parenting advice
to fiction. *The Locket's Secret* is
her first novel for young people.

*If you enjoyed
The Locket's Secret,
you'd probably like to
meet Anna Mei!*

Step into the daily life
of Anna Mei Anderson, a typical
American almost-teen adopted
from China as a baby. Anna Mei's
ups and downs are familiar bumps
in the road—the challenges every
kid encounters and navigates.
But as Anna Mei grows, she
learns just how much she can
count on her family, friends—
and her Catholic faith—for
guidance and support.

*Check out Anna Mei's
continued adventures in*

Anna Mei, Cartoon Girl,
Anna Mei, Escape Artist,
and Anna Mei, Blessing in Disguise.

CATHOLIC FICTION

Pauline Teen brings you books you'll love! We promise you stories that:

☑ make you laugh—and sometimes cry

☑ make you think and help you dream

☑ let you explore the real world

At Pauline, we love a good story and the long tradition of Christian fiction.* Our books are fun to read. Plus, they help you to engage your faith by accepting who you are *here and now* while inspiring you to recognize who God *calls you to become.*

*Think of classics like *The Hobbit, The Chronicles of Narnia, A Christmas Carol, Ben Hur,* and *The Man Who Was Thursday.*

A Catholic Place for Kids

Your school may have hosted a JClub Catholic Book Fair. But did your know that you can go to

www.jclubcatholic.org

for stories, gmes, saints, activities, prayers, and even jokes!

JClub is where faith and fun are friends.

Who: The Daughters of St. Paul

What: Pauline Teen—linking your life to Jesus Christ and his Church

When: 24/7

Where: All over the world and on www.pauline.org

Why: Because our life-long passion is to witness to God's amazing love for all people!

How: Inspiring lives of holiness through: APPs, digital media, concerts, websites, social media, videos, blogs, books, music albums, radio, media literacy, DVDs, ebooks, store, conferences, bookfairs, parish exhibits, personal contact, illustration, vocation talks, writing, editi...

BOOKS & MEDIA

The Daughters of St. Paul operate book and media centers at the following addresses. Visit, call or write the one nearest you today, or find us at www.pauline.org

CALIFORNIA
3908 Sepulveda Blvd, Culver City, CA 90230   310-397-8676
935 Brewster Avenue, Redwood City, CA 94063   650-369-4230
5945 Balboa Avenue, San Diego, CA 92111   858-565-9181

FLORIDA
145 S.W. 107th Avenue, Miami, FL 33174   305-559-6715

HAWAII
1143 Bishop Street, Honolulu, HI 96813   808-521-2731
Neighbor Islands call: 866-521-2731

ILLINOIS
172 North Michigan Avenue, Chicago, IL 60601   312-346-4228

LOUISIANA
4403 Veterans Memorial Blvd, Metairie, LA 70006 504-887-7631

MASSACHUSETTS
885 Providence Hwy, Dedham, MA 02026   781-326-5385

MISSOURI
9804 Watson Road, St. Louis, MO 63126   314-965-3512

NEW YORK
64 West 38th Street, New York, NY 10018   212-754-1110

PENNSYLVANIA
Philadelphia—relocating   215-676-9494

SOUTH CAROLINA
243 King Street, Charleston, SC 29401   843-577-0175

VIRGINIA
1025 King Street, Alexandria, VA 22314   703-549-3806

CANADA
3022 Dufferin Street, Toronto, ON M6B 3T5   416-781-9131